"You Have No Right to Destroy Me!"

Jan Martin cried as she tried to stop Antonio from extracting the last hairpin from her neat bun. She felt violated, stripped of her identity. Where was the naïve, plain girl from Kansas who had looked back at her from the mirror that morning?

Antonio laughed as he gazed at the lustrous waves of raven hair that tumbled over her shoulders. "I have no intention of destroying you." Then his expression changed swiftly to one of tantalizing devilment. "Or perhaps I do."

Suddenly he had her in his arms, his mouth close to hers, his breath hot on her skin. "Let's banish that prim, prissy Miss Martin, shall we?" he murmured hoarsely. "Let's kiss her good-bye forever."

MARY CARROLL
is an internationally known American writer who has published both here and abroad. She brings to her ~~~~~~~~~~ ack-ground of teac~~~~~~~~~~~~~~~~~~ er a unique insigh~~~~~

D1264414

Dear Reader:

Silhouette Romances is an exciting new publishing venture. We will be presenting the very finest writers of contemporary romantic fiction as well as outstanding new talent in this field. It is our hope that our stories, our heroes and our heroines will give you, the reader, all you want from romantic fiction.

Also, *you* play an important part in our future plans for Silhouette Romances. We welcome any suggestions or comments on our books and I invite you to write to us at the address below.

So, enjoy this book and all the wonderful romances from Silhouette. They're for *you!*

Karen Solem
Editor-in-Chief
Silhouette Books
P. O. Box 769
New York, N.Y. 10019

MARY CARROLL
Divide the Wind

Silhouette Romance

Published by Silhouette Books New York

America's Publisher of Contemporary Romance

Other Silhouette Romances by Mary Carroll

Shadow and Sun
Too Swift the Morning

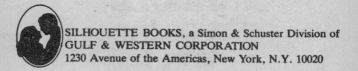

SILHOUETTE BOOKS, a Simon & Schuster Division of
GULF & WESTERN CORPORATION
1230 Avenue of the Americas, New York, N.Y. 10020

Copyright © 1981 by Annette Sanford
Map copyright © 1981 by Tony Ferrara

Distributed by Pocket Books

ISBN: 0-671-57075-7

First Silhouette printing April, 1981

10 9 8 7 6 5 4 3 2 1

America's Publisher of Contemporary Romance

Printed in the U.S.A.

Divide the
Wind

Chapter One

Still in a state of mild shock, Jan Martin slid into the back seat of the Rolls-Royce purring beside the main runway of the Milan airport and nervously straightened the skirt of her rumpled linen suit. She had dressed that morning in Paris expecting only her usual routine: six hours of sketching at the École de Mazarine, followed by a walk along the Seine and dinner afterward alone in her flat.

Instead, before noon she had been offered a fabulous job as a fabric designer with the prestigious firm Torelli Silks and had boarded a plane to Italy with its owner, the ruggedly handsome man at her side. It had been the most incredible—and the most alarming—day of her life.

From behind heavy-rimmed glasses Jan watched tensely as her sophisticated new employer said a few words to the liveried chauffeur in the front seat and then settled back beside her.

"Miss Martin—within half an hour we shall be in Como." Antonio Torelli's English was crisp and precise. "Before we arrive, I should like you to tell me everything about yourself."

A life history in thirty minutes? Jan looked despairingly at the craggy face so near her own. He had hardly spoken to her in Paris, choosing instead to channel most of his remarks concerning her employment through the design school's director. Their flight time he had spent at the bar discussing fluctuations in the Oriental market with a man dressed like an Indian prince. Why had he now, perversely, chosen this vulnerable moment of arrival to give her his undivided attention?

"I'm twenty-three," she began. "I'm an American."

"Yes, I know that," he said brusquely, "and also that you are from Kansas and for the past six months have been enrolled at the Ecole de Mazarine on a scholarship."

Beneath the gentle curve of her breast, Jan's heart beat like a caged bird's. Adjusting to the rarefied atmosphere of the Paris design school had been difficult enough for her. She had just begun to relax there—and now, plucked forth like an olive from a jar, she felt skewered on the tip of this urbane man's curiosity.

She took a quivering breath. "What else do you want to know?"

His mirthless smile barely hid his impatience.

"The lesser-known facts. Those details that are not printed on your record."

Tall and intense, the president of Torelli Silks was a singularly attractive man. Thirty, Jan guessed, or thirty-five. Eyes of a startling purple-blue peered out with uncompromising directness from beneath a heavy brow. Above his ears, silver wings of premature gray swept back and blended with a pepper-and-salt effect into the thick shock of hair that covered the rest of his well-shaped head. An aristocratic nose divided the rugged planes of his face. His jaw, set now, was firm and angular.

Beneath Jan's nervousness her fingers itched to draw him. His profile appeared as if it might have been lifted from a Roman coin, and beneath his excellently tailored suit—of Torelli silk, no doubt—his shoulders were as wide as those of a gladiator.

"I was orphaned at ten," she recited as if under a spell. "I grew up in the home of an aunt—Elizabeth McHenry—and this is my first time abroad."

He looked at her keenly. "No former husbands or fiancés?"

"No." Her answer was automatic, but his question had been unexpected—and in her mind it raised questions of her own. . . . Was he married? . . . Would she be seeing much of him? . . . But he was continuing.

"Is your aunt married?"

"My aunt is dead, Mr. Torelli."

"I see." His disturbing blue eyes moved over her as if he were searching a length of fabric for flaws. "How do you spend your leisure time?"

Jan drew her lips together, annoyed at this further intrusion into her personal life. "I read. And I draw."

Suddenly he produced the same dazzling smile that had tipped in his favor the balance of her hesitation that morning. "You draw very well. Exceptionally well. I expect great things of you."

"Please don't!" Jan's gray eyes widened. "Not yet, at least." Of all the alarming aspects this abrupt change in her life promised to entail, she found Antonio Torelli's unqualified confidence in her abilities the most upsetting. "I warned you this morning—I may not stay."

The smile vanished, and Antonio Torelli surveyed her coolly, a tiny muscle rippling in his angular jaw.

"As you recall," she went on quickly, "I've come prepared to stay only a week—or ten days at the most." He had not come with her up the six flights to her flat when she had gone to collect her things after the bargain had been made, but it was plain now from the look he turned on her that he was of the opinion that whatever she had packed into the scuffed suitcase the driver had stowed in the trunk of the car was probably all she had.

He wasn't far from wrong.

Jan lifted her chin. "I agreed to consider your offer because at the end of the month my scholarship expires, and I need the money. But I won't stay if I'm not sure I can do the work. I hope you understand that."

"Oh, I do indeed." His sharp glance probed her uneasy gray eyes behind the heavy glasses. "If such proves to be the case, I shall be the first to suggest that we terminate our agreement."

"Fine," said Jan, but her mouth went dry at the thought of such a possibility. She did desperately need at least a few months of the fantastic salary Torelli was offering. If only she could merit it. She sketched such simple things—leaves, flowers—and her daydreams, of course. Those flowing, swirling flights of fancy that translated themselves on paper as magical abstracts. But how would they print out on cloth? Only time would tell, and she felt so tense now that she wondered if—catapulted as she had been into this strange new environment—she would ever again feel relaxed enough to daydream.

"What do you know about the silk business?" he said abruptly.

"Nothing." *Strike two,* she thought.

But Torelli seemed pleased by her answer. "Good. You do not come to us with any misconceptions, then—or any previous commitments?" His gaze went through her like a saber.

She shook her head, wondering at the same time what he meant. What a strange man he was, she thought with a shiver. Affable one moment and cold as steel the next. But terribly attractive, provided one admired suave, self-assured men—which she did not. Life under the supercritical eye of a maiden aunt had done little to bolster her own self-esteem, and a surplus of self-confidence in others always put her on her guard.

She braced herself for further inquiries into her personal history, but when none were forthcoming she glanced at Torelli again and discovered that his attention seemed focused, not on her, but on the back of the chauffeur's cap. He seemed to have forgotten her entirely.

Oddly let down, Jan pulled her gaze away, annoyed that she could not erase from her mind's eye his image, particularly his mouth—the sensuously full bottom lip; the firm, straight upper one. Together the two appeared almost as separate sides of the man himself: one erotic, impetuous, and hotly passionate, and the other cold, calculating, almost cruel. Unable to restrain herself, she stole another look at him. Which side was dominant?

He felt her gaze and swung his head around. For a moment they stared at each other, Jan cringing under the look he gave her. She knew what he must be thinking. *What a drab thing this girl from Kansas is, with her thick-rimmed glasses, and her tightly knotted hair, and her undistinguished features.*

Jan thought the same thing whenever she caught sight of herself in mirrors or shopwindows. She was too plain for words, too spinsterish as Aunt Elizabeth had been, too shy and reserved for anyone to consider her interesting, much less desirable in a sexual way.

She blushed, aware that Antonio Torelli's presence on the seat beside her had set her thinking along lines she usually suppressed. She settled deeper into her corner and concentrated her attention on the emerald terraces coming into view as they approached the city of Como. She shouldn't have come, but probably within a week she would be on her way back to Paris anyway. Then what?

Another dismal secretarial job until she could land a renewal of her scholarship? Employment at Torelli Silks was the opportunity of a lifetime, but she feared there wasn't much chance she had the personality to hang on to it—or perhaps the talent, either, although she was surer of herself on that score than on any other. She was a competent artist, she knew, or the Ecole de Mazarine would never have admitted her. But projecting her abilities into a salable commodity—ah, there was the rub.

"We shall tour the mills first," she heard Torelli say in his clipped, precise English. "Before you begin your work you should have a clear concept of looming and silk screening."

"Silk screening," said Jan. "I'm familiar with that." She expected Torelli to be pleased, but to her dismay she saw that her words had produced the opposite effect.

"Then you misled me when you pretended ignorance about our operations," he accused.

She shrank from his menacing tone. "Not at all. I know about silk screening from the work I've done in Paris. But the way silk is manufactured, that sort of thing—I know nothing about that, as I said."

"Most of our raw silk comes from the Orient. Its manufacture is unimportant as far as you are concerned." His purple-blue eyes riveted her into her corner. "The thing of most importance is that you realize that our designs are the same as gold to us. We guard them as fiercely as one would a great treasure, and we do not take lightly any breach of faith on the part of our employees."

"I can understand that." In Jan's opinion there

was too much these days of telling tales out of school. When she browsed in bookstores she scrupulously avoided those best sellers that professed to "tell all" about public figures who, it seemed to her, had a right to expect the strictest loyalty from their employees. "That's quite a sensible policy."

Antonio received her comment with a cold stare. "I'm pleased you approve."

Jan bit her lip. Now he thought her impertinent! Floundering for a safe topic, she seized on the nearest thing—the terraced slopes beyond the window. "Oh!" She pointed them out. "Vineyards."

Torelli gave a disgusted snort. "You find vineyards remarkable?"

Jan flushed, more angered than embarrassed. Antonio Torelli awed her, but she had never appreciated rudeness, no matter who displayed it. "They are remarkable to one accustomed to wheatfields and prairies," she answered tightly. "Until I came to France I had never seen a vineyard. Have you ever seen a wheatfield, Mr. Torelli?"

He frowned. "Not a Kansas wheatfield, Miss Martin."

"What a pity." She folded her hands primly in her lap. "In summer they are quite spectacular."

"Oh?" At her show of spirit a corner of his mouth twitched. "Golden, I would imagine, and lyrical, as they undulate in the relentless Plains wind."

Her head came around. "You *have* been to Kansas!"

"Only in the pages of books." She saw the glitter of amusement that appeared in his remarkable eyes. "You have studied silk screening, Miss Martin." His

14

shoulders lifted in a shrug. "I have studied American geography."

Without intending to, Jan smiled. She liked him, she realized with a shock. He was curt and arrogant and rude. He was overly self-assured and probably a snob—but she liked him.

She might as well admit, too, that the planes of his face excited her. She was attracted to his strength and to the glimmers of laughter that now and then surfaced in those oddly colored eyes that were the rich hue of wild mountain asters—or of the mountains themselves, distant in a twilight haze—

Suddenly she was aware that she was staring at him, and she felt a rush of color staining her cheeks.

"You read and you draw," he said, "but I think you also enjoy analyzing other people."

Her color deepened. "I do find other people interesting, yes."

"But you also find it difficult to tell them so." He inclined his head toward her, and the early afternoon sun drew flattering shadows across his tanned cheeks. "I think, Miss Martin, that you might be called a shrinking violet."

Jan dropped her gaze, wondering why she was not offended by that teasing glance that seemed bent on pulling even her darkest secrets from her. "It's true that I am often ill at ease, particularly," she heard herself saying, "among strangers."

His tone sharpened. "Why?"

How often she had pondered that herself! "I suppose by nature I am simply not outgoing unless I know someone well."

"I see." He folded his arms across his chest in a

manner that seemed to say that he considered that explanation quite satisfactory. "Certainly there are worse things."

Jan felt a surge of relief. Evidently she had passed one test at least. What would be the next?

But Antonio Torelli's curiosity where she was concerned had spent itself, it seemed. He leaned forward and gave the driver a few curt instructions in Italian and then settled back to stare out the window until the Como skyline came into view.

The silk houses of Como were dark, medieval buildings near the Piazza Cavour, the ancient square facing the lake and lined on its other sides by hotels and cafés. From her reading Jan was aware that Como was a city with two hearts—one that beat frivolously with the festive air of all resort towns, and the other a ponderously pounding heart that concerned itself only with business.

It was to this section of the city that Antonio took her, and inside the glowering old structures that housed his mills and his showrooms he revealed to her his world.

As relentless as a schoolmaster he led her through cavernous rooms filled with machines but manned with surprisingly few attendants.

"These are the most modern looms in the world," Antonio told her proudly, pointing out that for every dozen machines only one operator was needed.

"Of course," he went on, "we must still maintain a certain number of the old box looms for our specialties—crepe de chine, silk velvets, tapestries."

He eyed her sharply. "Do you know of our tapestries?"

"I have read about them," she answered with her heart in her throat, aware that if he quizzed her she would fail miserably. She was so befuddled by the maze he had led her through and the mass of statistics he had thrown at her that she could hardly remember her name. Numbly, she followed him into the next building, vowing to improve her concentration.

Soon, however, she realized she was far more interested in the man than in what he was saying. She noticed the respect he commanded everywhere and the looks of longing the young mill girls fastened on him as he passed by. She could understand those looks. He was an enormously appealing man. Virile, athletic-looking, keenly intelligent—and totally committed to the silk business. If he had a wife, Jan thought as she trailed after him, it must be difficult for her to compete with such an all-consuming interest. In only two hours he had exhausted her with his enthusiasm and the endless stream of information he so effortlessly spouted.

However, when they finally emerged into the showrooms, Jan revived quickly. Unlike the clinical severity of the mills, the showrooms were opulent quarters designed to point up public relations and marketing.

Everywhere bolts of finely woven silks were displayed. There were luxuriously furnished conference rooms, and carpeted lounges large enough for the serving of luncheons while style shows were in progress. There was the latest communications equipment for instant contact with all points of the world market, and cozy little areas where clients could relax with drinks and conversation.

But dominating everything else were the miles of cloth the mills were incessantly producing. Jan was enthralled by the vibrant colors that met her eye on every hand, but at the core of her wonder was a nagging anxiety. The sophisticated designs she was viewing were so far removed from the sort of work she was accustomed to doing that she found it impossible to imagine how she would ever fit in at Torelli Silks.

With a leaden heart she listened as Antonio pointed out pridefully one whole wall filled with awards and citations his designers had won for the company through the years. He seemed oblivious to her mounting tension until they reached the final showroom. From there he led her off into his private office where he motioned for her to be seated in one of two leather chairs that faced his imposing desk. Then, suddenly, he pinpointed her with narrowed blue eyes.

"You look exhausted, Miss Martin."

"I'm overwhelmed, Mr. Torelli," she answered faintly. "You have a fantastic layout here, but—"

His gaze hardened. "But what, Miss Martin?"

She sighed helplessly. "I won't know how to work here."

"What do you mean?" He frowned. "If you are concerned that your working accommodations will be inadequate—"

"No, no, it isn't that." She had looked enviously

at the neat, airy designer studios he had pointed out, each one filled with the clear Italian light that fell through the skylights onto elevated drawing tables. There was no question that the finest working conditions prevailed at Torelli Silks. *But what if one had no ideas?* What if what one produced was not competitive with that of the dozens of smart-looking young persons she had seen bent intently over their sketches?

Torelli continued to stare at her. "What is it, then?"

Her throat tightened. "The silks you showed me." She took a trembling breath. "They were marvelous—wonderfully sophisticated creations. I can't produce anything like that."

From across the desk he looked at her calmly. "I don't expect you to."

"Why have you hired me, then?"

A shadow of annoyance crossed his darkly handsome face. "Certainly not to create more of what I already have too much of."

"But whatever I do, it will have to meet your standards of excellence," she persisted.

"Indeed it will."

"Well, that's it, don't you see? I have so little training—"

"I was not attracted by your training, Miss Martin." Slender fingers that belied their strength pyramided beneath his aquiline nose. "I was attracted by your originality. By the sensitivity in your work."

As upset as she was, Jan felt a glow of pride. She

was not unaware that the drawings she had submitted week after week at the Ecole de Mazarine had elicited admiration for their subtle simplicity and depth of feeling, but she had not imagined that a businessman of Torelli's scope would count such things valuable. She said timidly, "How can you be sure those qualities will prove useful here?"

"It's my business to be sure," he answered firmly. "I should not have employed you if I had had any doubts. All that is required is that you produce the finest work you are capable of, and we shall have no problems."

Jan swallowed. "I hope you're right."

"I can't afford to be wrong," he said and pushed back from his desk. Jan noticed as he stood that the lean strength of his body matched his self-assurance. "Now," he said decisively, "enough of instructions—and of uncertainties, too," he added pointedly. "It's time we relaxed over dinner."

"Dinner?" Jan looked up at him blankly. The clock on the desk showed not quite six—too early, she would imagine, for a man of Antonio Torelli's Continental tastes to dine. And even if it were not, surely he couldn't mean to take her with him.

But he meant exactly that. He towered over her, his amused, magnetic glance lifting her from her chair. "Come along. You must be starving."

She was, and she was thrilled that he had invited her, but she answered without hesitation. "It's kind of you to include me in your plans, but I'm afraid I'm not properly dressed."

"On the contrary," he said sardonically, his eyes moving over the prim linen suit she wore. "Proper is the very word I would have chosen." Then, with an authoritative air that left no room for refusal, he steered her out into the waning light of the Italian evening.

Chapter Two

A sleek little sports car waited at the curb for
Antonio and Jan when they came out of the showroom office, and though Jan wondered where the
Rolls-Royce had gone and where it had taken her
suitcase, she climbed obediently inside when Antonio opened the door for her and settled herself on
the leather seat. His hand on her arm had awakened
a pleasant excitment within her that persisted as she
watched him come around the car. Inspired by that
and reassured by his renewed vote of confidence, she
allowed herself to enjoy a feeling of optimism.

Perhaps things would work out after all . . . and if
they did— She cast a hopeful glance at Antonio as he
slid beneath the wheel. If they did work out, the
possibilities here might be limitless.

While they drove, Antonio pointed out places
of interest, most of which Jan was familiar with

from her reading. It was thrilling to see them for the first time, but Antonio at her side distracted her.

She was increasingly intrigued by him. He was domineering and aggressive and at times excruciatingly blunt—and yet flashes of boyish appeal that showed unexpectedly in his behavior endeared him to her. The romance in her life up to now had been largely confined to the pages of books. Few interested males had braved Aunt Elizabeth's rigid scrutiny a second time. Also, Jan suffered from a suffocating sense of inadequacy in any situation that seemed to her to demand feminine wiles. Flirting made her feel idiotic, and to behave as if she were hanging on every word a man spoke disgusted her.

But now, seated beside a man who could easily have stepped from the pages of the romantic novels that she avidly read during her evenings alone, she found her imagination soaring. While he talked, she looked at the buildings he pointed out, but in her mind's eye she pictured herself in his arms or caressed by the hand that lay lightly on the steering wheel. . . .

Antonio broke into her daydream. "The cathedral of Santa Maria Maggiore," he said, pointing to the left.

Jan shifted her gaze quickly. "Oh, yes—I've read about it." Reciting from the storehouse of her memory, she said, "The two statues in front are Roman senators, aren't they?"

Antonio looked at her. "Pliny the Elder and the Younger," he answered dryly.

"I thought so," she said, pleased she could show him how well informed she was about his country, but her smile faded when she saw his scowl. Evidently a well-informed woman was not to his taste. Silently she vowed to keep to herself any further comments that might emphasize her bookishness, and for a time she was able to sit quietly, nodding when he spoke and refraining from any remarks of her own.

But on the outskirts of the city, Antonio turned off into a parklike area of manicured lawns and carefully clipped shrubbery. Jan looked around and then sat forward eagerly, excitement rising in her chest. "What is this place?"

"The Villa d'Este," he said, naming with noticeable pride a sixteenth-century royal villa turned hotel that, Jan remembered, had for the last hundred years been renowned for its Old World grandeur and luxuriant surroundings.

"The Villa d'Este!" she exclaimed. "I was sure it was. Yes—look! There's the waterfall and over there the formal gardens. Oh! And the *palace!*"

"You've read about it, of course," he said darkly.

"At least a hundred times! I think it's one of the most romantic places in Europe." She turned to him with shining eyes. "This isn't where you're taking me to dinner, is it?"

"If you have no objections."

"I can't believe it! I'm actually going to dine here?"

Antonio's jaw hardened. "Why not?" Cutting the wheel sharply, he pulled into the parking area.

"We're hungry, they serve good food. It was the logical place to come."

"But the *Villa d'Este!*" she babbled on heedlessly. "It's the most exclusive holiday oasis in Italy."

He shut off the motor and gave her a steely glance. "And you," he said curtly, "are a designer for the most exclusive silk house in Italy. Your humble gushings are unbecoming in one who holds such a position."

Shocked into numbness, Jan watched as he came around the car and opened the door for her. She began an apology. "I only meant—"

But he cut her off. "I am quite aware of what you meant. That, I'm afraid, is the problem." The blue eyes stared at her with icy condescension. "Are you coming or not?"

Wordlessly she followed him up a graveled path, her face on fire from his rebuke. When they reached a flowered archway, he stepped aside and she passed in front of him into a garden where dainty little tables were laid and elegantly attired couples sat chatting and sipping drinks.

It was a setting straight out of the romantic literature she loved so well, but the pleasure she would normally have found in it had been spoiled by Antonio's outburst, and she wished with all her heart she were back in Paris in her sixth-floor apartment with a sandwich and a book.

When they were seated beside an enormous pittosporum that breathed its orange-blossom fragrance across their table, Antonio spoke again in his crisp, precise way. "You may have considered my remark rude just now, but it was necessary, I think, to point out to you a rather serious fault."

How kind of you! Jan thought bitterly, struggling to maintain what little composure she had left.

He went on with airy confidence. "You see, when one is too—"

But Jan cut him short with an angry hiss. "Will you stop it! If you had in mind to scold me, you might at least have had the grace to do so in your office."

"Scold you?" Antonio regarded her with a look of pained astonishment. "My dear young woman, don't be so thin-skinned. I observed an unattractive tendency you have of demeaning yourself—a slight character fault, you might say—and I merely offered a bit of constructive criticism."

"My *character!* You feel qualified to criticize that when you never laid eyes on me until you burst into my classroom this morning and snatched me up like a box of soap powder?"

Two bright spots of color appeared high on Torelli's cheekbones. "What a firecracker you are," he said coldly. "I shall make a point of remembering not to light the fuse again in public."

Jan's chin trembled. "Don't trouble yourself. I shan't give you another opportunity. I should like to return to Paris tonight, please."

The blue eyes narrowed. "I shall certainly not allow that. We made an agreement. You have an obligation to me to at least remain here through the trial period."

"I agreed to draw fabric designs—not to submit to your insults."

Antonio folded his arms across his wide chest. His jaw tightened as he fixed his gaze on an indefinite spot across the garden. "Miss Martin—I had no intention of insulting you. If it appears to you that I did, you are mistaken. Now—will you have a glass of wine, or shall we go directly in to dinner?"

Jan stared at him in angry helplessness. She wanted nothing he offered, but she had no suitcase, no money for plane fare, and no idea how to get back to Como or where to go if she got there. "Wine, please," she said in a choked whisper, vowing that if he forced her to eat she would throw the plate at him.

Antonio summoned a waiter. "Corvo di Salaparuta in chilled glasses," he said curtly. "And bring the menu when you return."

They sat in total silence until the wine had been set in front of them and Antonio had unfolded the elaborate menu. Without consulting Jan, he spoke again to the waiter.

"Cappeletti in broth, roast capon stuffed with chestnuts—and for dessert, cold zabaglione. See that we are served in the main dining room. The maître d' knows my table."

When the waiter had vanished, Jan glared across at Antonio. How could she ever have been fooled into thinking she liked this arrogant, overbearing stuffed shirt? She had never met anyone so disagreeable in her life.

But almost at once she was reminded of his powerful charm.

An elderly couple passing their table halted and turned back with delighted exclamations. "Tony!"

The white-haired man put out his hand. "I'd given up hope of seeing you this trip. Your office informed me you were out of the country."

Antonio sprang up. "Roberto! I've just returned today from Paris. Angela, my dear—hello!" He embraced the aging but beautiful woman who stood smiling fondly at him. "What a fortunate meeting this is!" Proudly he turned to Jan. "You must meet my new designer, Jan Martin." And then, as if they were intimates, he reached out and took Jan's hand, bringing her to her feet. "May I present two dear friends of long standing from Venice, Jan—Roberto and Angela Mignelli."

Mignelli Lace? Jan wondered, dazed by Antonio's swift change of disposition and made tongue-tied by the prominent pair before her.

But at once the older woman captivated her with her graciousness. "What a pleasure it is to meet you, my dear. But do sit down again. You mustn't let us interrupt. The Villa d'Este is a most charming place for two young people to enjoy each other. Nothing should be allowed to spoil your evening."

Antonio spoke quickly. "Angela, my dear, you are incapable of spoiling anything. Everything you touch, you enhance. Come—" He pulled out chairs. "You must both sit down. You must have a drink with us."

But the Mignellis declined. They were on their way back to Venice, they explained. "However, we shall look forward to seeing you again," Angela said privately to Jan as Roberto and Antonio engaged for a moment in conversation. "Ever since Tony spoke of you in the spring we've been eager to meet you.

I'm certain that you will be a tremendous help to him in the war he is waging." Oblivious to Jan's astonished stare, Angela gave her a kindly pat. "Do your best for him, won't you, my dear? Torelli Silks is too precious an institution to be undermined by traitors."

When the Mignellis were gone, Antonio, in a much improved mood, turned back to Jan. "Shall we go into the dining room now?"

Jan eyed him stonily. "What did Signora Mignelli mean by saying that I am to help in the war you are waging?"

Antonio blinked. "Angela said that?"

"She also said you had mentioned my name to them in Venice—in the *spring.*"

He recovered his composure. "Perhaps I did, but we won't discuss it now."

"I think we should."

"The subject is upsetting. I prefer we enjoy our dinner."

"I'm not hungry."

Antonio laid a firm hand on her chair. "Your appetite will return when you have tasted what I have ordered."

"Mr. Torelli—I want the answers to my questions."

He smiled suddenly, the bewitching smile that twice today had rendered her powerless to oppose him. "And you shall have them. But now you must have pity on our waiter. Look—do you see how he is almost standing on his head?" he said jovially. "He is trying to tell us that our capon is ready and that unless we go along at once it will be colder than the

29

zabaglione." Antonio pulled out her chair. "Afterward we shall talk."

Jan was determined that not a morsel of food would get past her lips, but once inside the villa's main dining room she succumbed almost at once to the Old World elegance that prevailed everywhere. Against a background of Viennese waltzes, Antonio began a fascinating discussion of the Mignellis Venetian residence, and she learned that the couple were indeed the founders of the venerable Mignelli Lace Company. By the time their food had arrived, Jan had become absorbed in the interesting account of how they had taken their business underground while Mussolini was in power during the Second World War, and, forgetting the antagonism Antonio had aroused in her earlier, she ate with pleasure.

Once again she came under the spell of the compellingly sensuous man speaking animatedly across the table—a fact that alarmed her more than she cared to admit. *His attractiveness was purely superficial,* she told herself sternly. That aristocratic head, she must remember, was filled with conceit.

Nevertheless, by the time they had finished their dinner, she was laughing at his witticisms, and when several heads turned in their direction as they left the dining room, she felt a glow of pride that this indisputably handsome man had chosen to bring her to such a fascinating place.

He had not been at all embarrassed by her rumpled linen suit and plain appearance, she mused, but had introduced her to his friends with pride. He had even taken her hand! In the dim interior of the car she flushed, remembering the pressure of his strong fingers. A swift fantasy engaged her . . . *He found her plain, scrubbed looks appealing . . . he had always admired quiet, retiring women who at heart were as spirited as firecrackers . . .*

She jumped as his low-pitched voice brought her back to reality. "Are you comfortable? Or shall I turn on the heater?"

"I'm quite warm, thank you." She waited a moment, hoping he might save her the embarrassment of reopening the issue he had postponed with dinner, but he only said, "We'll be driving for a while. Let me know if you get too cool."

Chapter Three

They had been on the road for nearly ten minutes when Jan, bolstered by the tune Antonio was humming softly beneath his breath, dared to inquire: "My questions, Mr. Torelli—shall we discuss them now?"

The humming broke off abruptly. "If you like."

She hesitated. "Then I should like to know about the war Signora Mignelli mentioned."

She saw a muscle jump in his cheek, but he said promptly, "War is exactly what it is. Torelli Silks is fighting for its life."

Jan, who had anticipated evasiveness, was startled. Surely he was exaggerating.

"What I showed you this afternoon is the impressive facade of what is at the moment a quite shaky business," he went on grimly. "Not that we are in imminent danger of going under or declaring bank-ruptcy—or that we ever will be." His jaw hardened. "But for the first time in our history we are not the leader in our field."

"How can that be?" Jan was wide-eyed. "Your company is known all over the world and has been for more than half a century. Why, I've read—"

"In this instance," he broke in sharply, "every-thing you have read is outdated. The picture has changed drastically, and it happened overnight." Jan saw his sensuous lower lip jut forward defiantly. "When I discover who is to blame, heads will roll, I can promise you that."

"This seems incredible," whispered Jan. *More so,* she thought dazedly, *because the self-assured Antonio Torelli was confiding in her!*

"To put it plainly," he went on, "someone is stealing our designs and distributing them through-out the market." The car reached a fork in the road. Antonio turned away from Como, but Jan scarcely noticed. "Two designs that were certain to have been prizewinners—and, more important, would have sold to the finest couture houses in France—appeared last week in bolts of silk arriving on the Continent from Thailand. Others have turned up as mass-market prints from your country, and still others at silk houses in Como."

Jan stared. "Designs produced in your studios by your designers? But what do the designers say? How do they account for this?"

"They are as bewildered as anyone—or so it would appear. I've had them all on the carpet. We've gone over every step in the design process, listed everyone who has any opportunity at all for copying the designs. Everything and everyone check out, and still the thievery goes on."

"It is known that these are your designs that are being improperly distributed?"

Antonio's nostrils flared. "Among professionals? Of course."

"Then isn't it unethical for your competitors to deal in stolen goods?" Jan protested.

"Unethical, yes—but also good business. Besides, we are dealing to a great extent with ideas. No substantial proof exists that the designs were originally ours—though I know they were, and I'm fairly certain those who are making use of them know it, too. But, as you say, they are competitors. Any one of them would welcome a chance to assume the position that Torelli Silks has always enjoyed in the world market. Some of them, in fact," he added with a note of outrage, "are already doing just that."

Jan sat back. *I am to help in this war?* The idea was preposterous. Had Antonio fired all his staff? Was he starting over now with a fresh crew? Surely not. That would hardly be fair to those who were innocent. Or perhaps—

Suddenly a thought occurred to her, and in mute astonishment she stared across at her companion.

Antonio went on talking, but for Jan his words ran together without meaning. This afternoon he had told her that she had a special talent, an originality he prized. Won over by his praise, she had allowed herself to be convinced.

But now, with these amazing revelations ringing in her ears, his eagerness to bring her to Italy assumed an entirely different aspect. *She had been right in her hesitancy to accept his offer,* she thought, feeling suddenly ill. It wasn't her talent he was interested in—it was her ordinariness, her lack of sophistication.

Her face burned. No wonder he hadn't minded her shabby attire this evening . . . or been put off by escorting one as unglamorous as herself to the exclusive Villa d'Este. *Her unattractiveness was what he was buying.* He had come to Paris seeking a dupe, a pushover, to bait his thieves—and in plain Jan Martin from Iona Corners, Kansas, he had found exactly what he was looking for!

Yes—that explained everything. *He planned to use her as his decoy.*

Her imagination shifted into high gear. No doubt he would make a great show—as he had done tonight before the Mignellis—of presenting her everywhere as his fabulous new discovery. When the word spread, whoever was stealing from him would take one look at her clothes, her hair, her bookish appearance, and realize at once how simple it would be to steal from her. *Do your best for Tony,* Angela Mignelli had whispered. How delighted that elegant woman must have been to see how well Antonio's dowdy choice fit her role!

Jan's gaze leaped to Antonio, whose eyes were intent on the winding road the car was following through the dark Italian landscape. Her lips parted. First she would insist that he return her at once to Paris, and then that he see to her immediate reinstatement at the Ecole de Mazarine.

But, like a specter, the scene she intended to

create rose and silenced her. Whom would the director believe? A green, whining girl? Or the scion of Torelli Silks?

Panicked, she licked her lips and considered her options. There were only two. She could go ahead and create a furor in Paris and end up with nothing, or she could stay on, draw her handsome salary, and play the fool.

Her eyes went back to Antonio at the wheel, speaking derisively now of the cutthroat practices of big business. Her heart hammered as she thought of the ridiculous fantasies she had indulged in earlier. She would hardly find her role difficult if she did decide to stay—playing the fool was for her second nature!

But how would Antonio handle this plot he had hatched? She stared across at him. Even as confident as he was about everything else, how could he be certain he could trust a stranger when someone he knew well was betraying him? He had humiliated her this evening, but, she thought with grim satisfaction, he must be doubly humiliated himself at having to stake the survival of his precious kingdom on one for whom he had so little regard—one too easily impressed with the things he took for granted and too quick to show anger when criticized.

Tears burned behind her eyelids. What was she doing here, riding through the night with this stranger who had dealt with her brutally and untruthfully? If she stayed, she would have to be constantly on guard. The thought exhausted her. She had lived a quiet, retiring life in Kansas until Aunt Elizabeth died, and even in Paris she had kept the bustling city at arm's length. She had no idea how she would react in the midst of intrigue.

But if she did stay, she thought with unexpected wistfulness, there might be other days like today, other excitements such as dinner tonight at the Villa d'Este and meeting the Mignellis. For the first time in her life she might have a chance to live as glamorously as the heroines in her books instead of only reading about them. Was it so wrong to wish for that?

There were other positive aspects, too, she reminded herself. Money was one. Her future was another. A record of employment at Torelli Silks would go well on her résumé, and if she did aid in catching the thief, Antonio was sure to be generous in his recommendation.

When Antonio left off speaking for a minute, she broke in tentatively. "Do the Mignellis know?"

Antonio picked up her train of thought. "About what's happening to the firm?"

"Yes." She squeezed her hands together in her lap. "And about the part I am to play."

"They've known since spring. That's what Angela meant when she told you I'd mentioned you."

"But you didn't know me then."

"I knew *of* you. I contacted the Ecole de Mazarine as soon as the fabric fair was over in late winter, and they sent me the qualifications of their most promising students."

Had they sent a description also? Jan wondered bitterly.

"It was at the fabric fair," said Antonio in a hard voice, "that I first discovered we were being robbed.

37

Our firm and a German one showed the same design."

Jan could sympathize with the embarrassment of that. As an artist she held creative integrity sacred. To have it flouted publicly was unthinkable. "What did you do?"

"I blew up, of course. Nothing like that had ever happened before. Naturally, I thought the German firm had pirated our work. I made some rather nasty accusations. Then it came out that the design had originated in the German studios. They produced documented proof. We, it seemed, were the pirates. We had no proof at all."

Jan stared at him. "You're saying the scheme works both ways, aren't you? That whoever is responsible either steals your designs and sells them to other companies, or else palms off on you—or on one of your designers—the work of another artist."

"That's the whole bloody business in a nutshell."

"Then why can't you discover who it is? What about the designer who made the duplication for the fair? She has to be guilty, doesn't she?"

Antonio sighed. "Unfortunately, it isn't that simple. In our firm we practice a pooling of ideas. Weekly sessions are held with all the designers present, as well as myself and one or two members of the board. We spend hours discussing trends. Then the designers submit anonymously whatever ideas have occurred to them. These are critiqued, sometimes added to, and sometimes tossed out. Those that survive are picked up by whichever designer feels she has the most to contribute, and the work goes on from there."

"So the design that turned up at the fair could have come from anyone in the group," said Jan. "That seems a terribly risky procedure."

"Certainly it has proven so in the last several months," Antonio agreed grimly. "But never before then. Pooling was the secret of our success, in fact. It provided a unique form of stimulation for the designers, and we believed that the mutual regard and trust it fostered made for a strong company. But now, because suspicion has replaced regard, we have become a weak company."

It was plain from Antonio's tone that weakness of any kind was to him intolerable.

"As soon as I could manage it after the fair," he went on, "I drove to Venice to consult with Roberto and Angela. In the life of their own firm they have weathered worse storms than this, and I wanted their opinion of my plan."

Jan could imagine what that plan was. "Did the Mignellis suggest that you employ me, Mr. Torelli?"

"Tony, please," he answered brusquely. "In the coming weeks we will be seeing a great deal of each other. I expect our relationship to be a close one, and formality will be out of place between us."

Jan's heart beat faster. If only he could have spoken those words under different circumstances! But said now in that businesslike tone, they only reinforced her suspicions that he had hired her to bait his trap. "Please answer my question," she said stiffly.

He gave her a wry glance. "Never one to be sidetracked, are you, Miss Martin?"

"Jan," she replied coldly.

Unperturbed, he went on in his crisp, efficient way. "No, the Mignellis did not recommend you—or anyone else. The choice was mine, and I'll tell you what it was based on.

"I need a designer who has never worked for a silk company—preferably one who has never worked at all in commercial design—and I need someone with fresh, original skills and a special quality never before seen on the market. The Mignellis agreed with me that if I were fortunate enough to find such a person Torelli Silks might have a chance to regain its status. You are that person," he finished flatly.

Did she dare believe that?

With his usual self-assurance Tony continued. "There were others whose talents appeared comparable, who had suitable backgrounds. There were one or two I almost settled on, but then I came to Paris . . ." He turned a slightly quizzical look on Jan. "I saw your work, and the decision was made."

Jan's heart pumped wildly. Despite her certainty that he was flattering her, she could not deny that she was pleased.

"The drawings the director showed me were perfect in every respect. I especially admire that illusory sense your work projects. It's marvelous— just what I've been searching for. If you hadn't agreed to come with me this morning," he finished decisively, "I would have kidnaped you."

The contrast between what he was saying and what he must actually be thinking was too much for Jan. "How do you know I won't betray you, too?" she said harshly.

His head swung around. "That's a strange question."

"I've admitted that my finances are strained." She marveled at her own boldness. "How do you know I can't be bought off by one of your competitors?"

His eyes went back to the road. "I've studied your background," he said evenly, but Jan could see that his grip had tightened on the steering wheel. "I know all about you."

"Oh—then your questions this morning were just a way of checking up."

"For someone so reserved," he came back, with a sardonic inflection in his icy tone, "you exhibit a surprising tendency for creating friction."

Though she trembled inwardly, she said in a strong voice, "If I can surprise you in one respect, I may do so in others."

The look he gave her cut clear through to her backbone. "I very much doubt that. But if you should"—she felt his ominous tone like a hand shutting off her breath—"you had better make certain the surprises are pleasant ones."

Chapter Four

Opening her eyes the morning after her arrival in Italy, Jan took a few seconds to remember where she was. She looked at the circular-shaped room, the high ceiling, and the three tall windows letting in the pale dawn light. Then her gaze fell on a chair where her linen skirt lay neatly folded, and the memory of her dinner with Tony Torelli and the ride in darkness along the shore of Lake Como jarred her wide awake.

She sat up. This was the Villa Torelli—Tony's ancestral home in Bellagio at Lake Como's edge. They had arrived here after midnight, and when a maid had brought her over from the main house to this ancient stone tower beside a moat that was scarcely visible in the moonless night, her worn suitcase had already been unpacked and the sad components of her limited wardrobe were hanging in the closet and folded away in the sweetly scented drawers of this cozy bedroom.

Hugging her knees to her chest, she savored the delicious excitement of having spent the night in such a romantic place. Beyond the windows she could see a blend of soaring peaks and lush Mediterranean vegetation. The room itself contained all the comforts one might imagine in the imposing guest quarters of a Lombardian villa—a thick golden carpet, an ivory dressing table with mirror rimmed in diamond-shaped panes of stained glass, and a sofa and chairs covered in the same rich blue-and-white fabric that curtained the bed.

Visible through a passage beside the fireplace was a sparkling tiled bath complete with half a dozen crystal bottles of oil and perfume, and open shelves holding stacks of fluffy blue-and-white towels. Scores of potted plants, all in bloom, banked a sunken tub.

A hush lay over everything.

Eagerly Jan threw back the comforter that had covered her through the chilly night and, in her thin gown, padded barefoot to the windows. Leaning over a low sill, she saw reflected in the clear, cerulean water of the moat the high-peaked tower— with herself a quarter of the way up, framed in the center window—and above her another floor, a chimney, and a single turret outlined against the azure sky.

On the ground level, a low stone wall separated the base of the tower from the moat and joined it a few hundred yards away to a corner of the rustic, thick-walled structure that was the central building of the villa. In front of it a paved courtyard stretched, and on either side of that lay a labyrinth of gardens, parks, and lawns, bounded at their extremities by a tangled, almost tropical jungle. As if on signal, hundreds of birds suddenly began to sing.

Thrushes? Warblers?

Enchanted, Jan leaned farther out the window, her dark hair falling loosely away from her bare shoulders. Almost at once a male voice rang out from below.

"Hello up there!"

Jan's startled glance darted downward. On the other side of the moat stood Tony, dressed in jeans, with a canvas cape slung carelessly over one shoulder. At his side a handsome brown-and-white Borzoi wagged his tail. "You're up early," he called. "I imagined you'd sleep until noon."

Frozen where she stood, Jan struggled to find her voice. "I've always been an early riser."

"So have I." His gaze swept over her. "Would you care for breakfast?"

"I'd like tea," she said faintly.

"Dress and come down, then. I'll let Nappy run a while longer and wait for you."

Jan nodded and, still under his scrutiny, withdrew inside the window. *He'd gotten an eyeful!* she thought, blushingly inspecting her transparent nightgown. At least her hair had offered some protection from those piercing blue eyes, but what was exposed he'd gotten a clear view of.

She had gotten a clear view of him, too, she reflected as she pulled on her linen skirt. He looked dashing in that cape. Not every man could wear one, but Tony had looked even more virile and appealing than he had the day before in his elegantly tailored suit. Perhaps the mountain light was flattering . . .

Anxiously she peered into the mirror and began winding her hair into the tight knot that customarily bound it. There were no shadows beneath her gray eyes, she was relieved to see, nor any other traces of the weariness she had felt when she had finally fallen into bed. Her skin, fine-textured and creamy, was her best feature, she believed, and this morning a tint of roses—put there no doubt by the brisk nip in the air—highlighted her prominent cheekbones.

Gazing at herself, she absently withdrew her hand from the coil of hair and watched as the lustrous rope unwound itself across one shoulder. A sense of giddiness took hold of her—a feeling of wantonness—and she experienced a sudden and overwhelming desire to be someone else—anyone but bookish, reserved Jan Martin.

A man looked at me almost naked this morning. Her eyes glowed luminously in the mirror. *What did he think?* Lightly she trailed her fingertips over the swell of her breasts. The tip of her tongue came out and followed the curve of her lips. What if one day that man looked at her and said that she was beautiful? . . . What if behind her plain, spinsterish image he discovered the woman she really was . . . the woman whose erotic dreams often lingered for hours after she awoke . . . the woman whose one most frequent desire was to be crushed in the arms of someone she loved—and who loved her in return?

The sharp sound of Antonio's voice calling the Borzoi came up from the courtyard. The daydream shattered. Jan snatched up a handful of pins and with a few skillful twists secured her hair. Then, grabbing up her glasses, she raced toward the stairs.

Tony was waiting for her on the paved courtyard in front of the great house, and as she came toward him, his keen-eyed glance followed her prim step. Self-consciously she quickened it.

Since awakening she had thought only of the glamor of her surroundings and of Tony's interested appraisal when she leaned out the window. But under his current scrutiny, she remembered why he had brought her to Italy and she vowed anew to keep her emotions in check.

"Ah," said Tony when she came within speaking distance. "I see you are once again the proper Miss Martin."

Jan flushed, cringing beneath the laughter she saw in his eyes. "I hope I haven't kept you waiting."

"You have," he answered crisply, "but I've enjoyed the glorious morning."

"So have I," she said gratefully. "From the tower I could see for miles."

He opened the front door for her, and they moved into the foyer of the impressive mansion. "Could you see La Punta Spartivento?"

"I don't know. What is it?"

"My, my." He made a clucking sound. "You haven't read about it?"

Jan flushed under this sardonic implication. "I'm afraid not."

"It's Bellagio's main attraction. The Point That Divides the Wind. But perhaps it's better viewed from the upper story," he went on carelessly. "Your studio is there. Have you inspected it?"

Jan's lips parted. "My studio? What do you mean?"

But they had reached a sunny breakfast room toward the rear of the house, and Tony did not reply, pausing instead to have a word with the uniformed maid who stood beside the door, and then, as she vanished into the kitchen, drawing out a chair at the table for Jan.

"I've ordered a full American breakfast for you, to get you off on the right foot," he told her loftily. "Bacon, eggs"—he flashed an indulgent smile— "and tea—though tea is not as American as coffee, is it?"

"Perhaps not." Numbly Jan wondered how she, who ordinarily had only a hot drink and toast, would manage a complete meal at this hour of the morning. "Aunt Elizabeth always preferred tea."

Taking his seat, Tony turned up his remarkable blue eyes. "And did Aunt Elizabeth always wear her hair in a tight little knot?"

Jan felt her face go scarlet.

"Yours was quite an astonishing sight this morning, flowing down like a dark Rapunzel's tresses." His teasing tone intensified. "You should wear it that way more often."

"I find it an annoyance," murmured Jan, who felt hot all over, even to the soles of her feet.

He set his head to one side and surveyed her critically. "It needn't be, I should think. You could tie it back—or loop it up in some more becoming way."

Suddenly Jan was angry. Why must he always pick her to pieces? "I am quite satisfied with my hair just the way it is."

"I see." He shrugged. "Then certainly you are the one whom you must please."

Meaning what? thought Jan bitterly. That she had no one else to please? "Why did you say the upper story of the tower is to be my studio?" she said, barely able to suppress her irritation.

"Because it is." Now he was annoyed too, she saw. "You will do your work there."

"I'm not to have one of the studios in Como with the other designers?"

"You sound disappointed."

"Well, certainly I'm surprised. When you were showing me around yesterday—"

He broke in. "You thought you would be settled in Como?" His look was incredulous. "How could you be so silly as to think that, after what I told you last evening?"

She bit back a sharp reply. How could *he* be so silly as to think she could serve as a decoy way out here? "I'll be all alone at the villa, won't I?"

"Hardly." He laughed unpleasantly. "There are the servants. I'll be in and out. So will Maria, for that matter."

Something tightened in Jan's chest. "Your wife?"

"I have no wife," he answered curtly. "Maria Bertani is a friend. Her villa adjoins this one."

The maid came in with their food and for a few minutes Tony was occupied, serving their plates. *What an utter fool she was,* thought Jan as she watched him. Last night driving up from the Villa d'Este she had been so sure she had figured out everything perfectly. Tony would use her as a decoy among his other designers . . . the thief would try to take advantage of her inexperience and be caught. It was all so simple, so logical—and evidently so incorrect.

Tony spoke up sharply. "Why aren't you eating? You're too thin as it is."

Hastily Jan picked up her fork. "I was wondering why you think it best for me to stay here—in such a remote place."

"I'd hardly call Bellagio remote," he replied. Then, with his coffee cup in midair: "Why are you making so much of this? Are you uncomfortable in the quarters I've provided?"

"That isn't it," she said desperately. "Perhaps if you just told me straight out what you expect of me, then I would know where I stand."

He stared at her. "I've made that perfectly plain, I think. I want designs—hundreds of them. I want that exquisite quality I saw exhibited in your work in Paris, and I want the work done in absolute secrecy."

Secrecy. "That's why you've put me in the tower?"

"You make it sound as though I were the Black Prince from some medieval fairytale," he said irritably. "The tower suits our purposes perfectly. I would think you might understand that. You can sleep there, work there. You can even eat there if you choose. There's a small kitchen, a dining room. Food can be brought over or prepared there— whatever you like."

Jan looked at him. Was it possible that he had told her the truth to begin with? That he had actually hired her because he admired her work and not because she was plain, naïve Jan Martin from Kansas? She moistened her lips. If that were so, other things were possible, too. She remembered the way he had taken her arm coming out of the showroom . . . the way he had looked at her bare shoulders this morning . . .

She blinked, excitement crowding her throat. "I can cook. I'm an excellent cook."

He stopped buttering his toast. "Fine, wonderful. Cook, then. Stitch tea cozies, raise ginger cats. I couldn't care less what you do as long as you tend to your work properly."

All around her Jan heard the crashing of day-dreams.

In a strangled voice she said, "I see."

"Good." He spoke again, briskly. "Perhaps you wouldn't mind passing the jam, then."

Blindly Jan handed across the porcelain jam jar. Then, pushing her chair back, she said, "Excuse me, please."

His head came up. "You've hardly touched your breakfast."

"I'm not hungry."

He looked at her with growing annoyance. "Well, at least finish your tea. We should talk. Surely you have more questions."

"You've answered them all, thank you." Without looking back, she rushed from the breakfast room.

Chapter Five

Sun was slanting through the west window of the tower when Jan set aside her sketchbook and leaned wearily back from the table where she had spent most of the afternoon. While her fingers had been busy with pencils and chalks, her mind had replayed every moment she had spent with Antonio Torelli, particularly those moments at the breakfast table.

Her conclusion was that she had acted like an idiot from start to finish. Like some adolescent schoolgirl she had built the wildest of fantasies around her new employer. She smiled grimly, thinking how that would shock him. She had even thought for a split second this morning that he might have brought her to the Villa Torelli to seduce her. But worse than that—for a moment or two she had considered letting him!

At least now she had her head on straight. Tony's

bluntness had seen to that. Sighing, she went to the window and rested her forehead against its ancient wooden frame. *He couldn't care less what she did.* He had made that so plain that even hours later his words still stung, causing her to recall anew why most of her life she had kept her emotions hidden behind a façade of cool reserve. It kept people at a distance. Whenever you let them come close, Aunt Elizabeth had cautioned, they invariably hurt you.

Jan's eyes went out over the tops of the trees that surrounded the villa, and she saw that the blue waters of Lake Como flowed back on two sides from a lush green promontory that stretched beyond the tile rooftops of Bellagio. Was that what Tony had said she should look for? The Point That Divides the Wind? Perhaps one day she might go down and see for herself what made the place so special. She might, that is, if the Black Prince saw fit to free her for a few hours from this captive residence!

Then, immediately, she was repentant.

The tower was far from a prison. It was a magic place she had fallen in love with. If no other good came out of this venture into northern Italy, she had at least experienced the enchantment of this delightful temporary home.

She had not even thought about lunch, she had been so absorbed in exploring its every nook and cranny. Originally—she had decided—the guard of the moat must have occupied it. On the ground floor there were a tiny kitchen and dining area and a sitting room. A circular stairway wound from there up to the second floor where her bedroom and bath were, and then on up to this top story—her studio. It appeared that it had all recently been redone with care and excellent taste. The stone walls had been lightened to a creamy ecru, the furnishings were elegant, and the floors were all carpeted in the same soft gold as that of her bedroom—except up here in the studio where fine hardwood had been laid (perhaps years before, judging from its patina) and left uncovered. Also, this upper story was sparsely furnished, as if it might once have been a tiny ballroom. Around the fireplace was a grouping of chairs and a sofa, and over by the window was the long table where she had been working and a desk, but the rest of the room was empty, making it ideal for laying out her drawings and for pacing around whenever she needed to stir up her creative juices. She liked the tower even better than the airy studios in Como. She enjoyed solitude, and here she was guaranteed to have plenty of that.

Then almost at once the sound of footsteps refuted her assumption. She heard men's voices, and then Tony Torelli's handsome head appeared at the top of the stairs.

"Bring the things up here, Heinz," he called back over his shoulder when he saw her, and then he strode into the room like a king, glancing about for evidence that Jan had made herself at home. Settling his disturbing gaze on her annoyed countenance, he said, "What are you doing? Hiding?"

"I've been working," she told him, bristling with resentment. He owned the place, of course, but needn't flaunt the fact! Besides, he had turned these quarters over to her, and he needn't think he could intrude whenever he pleased. "Was there something you wanted?"

"Yes." He looked at her coolly. "I've brought over a hamper. You must eat something."

"I'm not hungry."

"I'm bored with that answer," he said curtly. "What do you think you are? A butterfly that can subsist on air and sunshine?" He turned to the servant who had followed him in with a covered basket. "Here, Heinz. Set it down over there by the window, and leave the wine. I'll open it myself when we're ready."

When the man was gone, Tony turned toward the table. "First, let's have a look at what you've been doing."

"It's nothing," said Jan quickly.

"You said you'd been working."

"But not seriously." She had paid scant attention to the lines flowing onto the paper during the long hours she had sat there berating herself, but, whatever shapes they had taken, she was sure she had rather he didn't see them.

Ignoring her, Tony picked up her sketchbook and turned the heavy pages, his practiced eye skipping over the lines Jan's pencils had made. All at once he paused. "What's this?"

"What?" Her heart came up in her mouth as he held out the pad.

"This intertwining of grape leaves and wheat." He scowled. "The forms are totally incompatible." Then, suddenly, his smile flashed. "And yet they work, by heaven! And work beautifully." His bright eyes challenged her. "What were you thinking of when you put these two together?"

Jan felt heat rising to her cheeks as she recalled drawing violets as well—shrinking violets that she had half hidden in the grape foliage. In a moment he would notice those, too, and have no doubt what she had been thinking! Quickly she took the pad from his outstretched hand and clasped it, closed, against her breast. "I was daydreaming," she murmured.

"What about?" His gaze was unreadable. "Really," he said after a minute, "you are the most extraordinary girl. I believe you were still mulling over that remark I made yesterday about the vineyards. Were you?"

Jan wanted to sink through the floor. "Maybe. I don't remember."

His curious stare lasted another instant. Then he said briskly, "Come—let's eat. I've been out riding and missed lunch myself. I'm starved even if you aren't."

Pulling out a chair at the table, he waited for her to sit down and then took a seat beside her. "Let's see what we have here." Lifting the lid of the hamper, he sniffed appreciatively. "Something with horseradish, I'll wager. And a red wine from Bardolino. Don't be shy," he instructed. "Dive right in. This is a picnic, don't you see?"

He was like a boy, thought Jan, munching on a butter-and-watercress sandwich and eyeing him covertly as he twisted the wine cork out. A handsome, devilish boy who with a single smile could make her forget how much she disliked him. What fun this could be if he weren't her employer as well, and she weren't tongue-tied with nervousness in his presence. She watched his strong, slender fingers tilting the wine bottle and then passing a glass to her. Her hand trembled as she took it. Their glances locked.

"Jan Martin," he murmured, "your insecurities are showing again."

Color flooded her cheeks.

Setting his glass down, he looked directly at her. "Why do I frighten you?"

It was on the tip of her tongue to deny that he did, but his strong, frank gaze stilled the lie. "Because you're so caustic!" she blurted out.

His brows came together. "What? What do you mean?"

"I never know what you're going to say—and when you do say it, it's always about something I've done wrong or said wrong." Now that she had started, she couldn't seem to stop. "I'm too humble. I don't eat enough. I ask too many questions, or I can't answer yours!"

He watched her as she spoke. Then, without so much as a flicker of an eyelash to warn her, he leaned over and kissed her squarely on the mouth.

"There," he said when she drew back, wide-eyed and astonished. "That's quite enough of that. Eat."

"You see!" Startled beyond amazement, she raged at him. "That's exactly what I mean! You ask why I'm afraid of you, and then, while I'm trying to tell you, you kiss me! And scare me half to death!"

He burst out laughing. "You deliciously funny thing—will you be quiet and finish your sandwich?" He held up his hand. "No—not another word. Eat until I tell you you can stop. Then we'll take our wine over to that couch by the fireplace and you may have the floor. I will expect you to talk then until your head rolls off." He chuckled again. "But not another word until you're properly fed."

Apprehensively, Jan sipped her wine. The meal had calmed her to the extent that she had even begun to appreciate the humor in the two of them solemnly staring at each other over sandwiches and fruit, but Tony's nearness had again aroused thoughts that fostered fantasies, and she watched nervously as he came to the couch and took a seat beside her.

"Begin," he said, consulting his wristwatch.

"Just like that?" Jan blinked. "What shall I talk about?"

"That's your problem," he answered severely. "You have the floor."

Chewing the corners of her lips, she tried not to think that his mouth had rested there a few minutes before. Seizing the first thing that popped into her mind, she said, "How did you know I didn't come to lunch?"

He folded his arms. "The cook told me."

"Oh." She cast about frantically. "Was this a ballroom once?"

He shook his head. "A practice room. My sister studied ballet. Go on," he commanded.

"No." She set her jaw as if she were once again resisting one of Aunt Elizabeth's cross-examinations. "It's your turn. You say something."

"Very well." He fastened his penetrating gaze on her. "Why did you jump up like a frightened hare this morning and dash off from the breakfast table?"

"Because you were rude," she shot back. "You made it quite plain that I am of no importance whatsoever except for the work I'm to do here."

"I see." His blue eyes glinted. "Of what importance would you prefer to be?"

She flushed. She'd never tell him that! "I should at least like to be thought of as something more than a machine that turns out drawings."

"If that were all I considered you to be, would I have gone to all the trouble to fetch you from France?"

"Shall I tell you why I thought you did?" she said with sudden daring.

"Please do."

Now she was terrified, but there was no turning back. "I had the idea—last night I had it—I know it's ridiculous now, but I thought you chose me to work for you because you wanted someone who—" She licked her lips, unwilling to describe herself in the way she was sure he must see her. "Someone whom your thief would find easy to steal from, and then you would guard my work, and when the thief made his move, you would catch him—her. Whoever it is."

The curious look that had come over his face while she spilled out her suspicions turned to blank amazement. "I would set you up, in other words."

"Yes." She flushed. "But then, when you told me I would be working here and not in Como, I realized I was mistaken."

"And you got your feelings hurt." He frowned. "You wanted to be set up?"

"No, of course not."

"Then I don't understand."

"Oh, neither do I," she said desperately. "Let's forget it, shall we?"

"We can't. Not until we've straightened the whole thing out."

"But it's very clear to me now," she said quickly. "The reason you've brought me here, I mean."

"Which is that I like your work. I told you that to begin with, so why did you go on with that half-cocked notion? Do you know what the whole trouble with you is?" His gaze pierced her. "You haven't the faintest idea of your own worth. That's what I meant last evening when I tried to make clear how unbecoming that air of false humility is."

"It is not false!"

"Oh, look here, now—you aren't going to tune up and cry again, are you?"

"I didn't cry!" she protested indignantly.

"You weren't two breaths from it. But to get on: What you must realize is that you are an exceptionally talented young woman. The world is your oyster. All that is required of you is that you accept that fact and enjoy it. Who ever gave you the idea that you have to go around apologizing for yourself?"

"I don't do that!"

"You do," he said sternly. "Was it your Aunt Elizabeth?"

"Don't speak unkindly of Aunt Elizabeth! When nobody else would, she gave me a home."

"Yes," he said dryly. "And I think she gave you a

capital case of inferiority to go along with it."
Suddenly he leaned forward and yanked off her
glasses. "Is she the reason you wear these hideous
things?"

Jan made an ineffective grab for them. "I wear
them so I can see!"

"I can't believe there aren't more attractive ones
available on the market." In disgust he tossed them
aside. "And that knot at the back of your head—"
His hand came out toward her hair. "I can't abide
it."

"Who's making me feel inferior now?" she demanded hotly, her hands flying to her hair, but not in
time to stop him from extracting the last pin.
Lustrous waves tumbled down over her shoulders.

"There!" He sat back and gazed with satisfaction
at the dark hair framing her tight lips in a white face.
"That's much better."

"Better for you, perhaps!" She felt violated,
completely stripped of her identity. "You haven't
left me a leg to stand on, have you? You don't like
my hair or my glasses—or even my aunt!"

"Don't be absurd," he answered calmly. "I never
knew your aunt."

"You don't know me, either—so you have no right
to destroy me!"

He laughed. "You say the most ridiculous things. I
have no intention of destroying you." Then his
expression changed swiftly to one of tantalizing
devilment. "Or perhaps I do."

Suddenly he had her in his arms, his mouth close
to hers, his breath hot on her skin. "Let's banish that

prim, prissy Miss Martin forever, shall we?" he murmured hoarsely. "Let's kiss her goodbye."

Jan struggled, but his lips closed over hers. They possessed first her mouth, then her whole being. Her own lips parted and she felt the teasing touch of his tongue. Her heart took a leap. Then, as quickly as the kiss had started, it was over. Jan lay still in his arms, faint with a mixture of ecstasy and disbelief.

"Most enjoyable," he murmured, nibbling at her lips again, but this time she stiffened, panicking.

Tony drew back, eyes full of laughter. "We couldn't quite do away with her, could we?"

"Who?" said Jan weakly.

"Miss Martin." With erotic slowness he pulled a fingertip across her lips. Then, chuckling softly, he released her and stood up. "But I think we gave her quite a fright."

At the head of the narrow, winding stairs, he turned, hands low on his hips, thighs taut in his close-fitting jeans. "You are not to stay shut up in this place day and night," he said in a commanding voice. "You are to get out and take long walks and tramp around the grounds and swim. I want some color in those cheeks. This evening at eight I will expect you in the solarium for cocktails and, afterward, for dinner." His gaze moved over her smock-clad figure poised tensely on the couch. "Wear a pretty dress and be there on time."

Chapter Six

Tony's invitation, coupled with the events of the afternoon, left Jan shaken and uncertain. For the tenth time she shoved the clothes hangers back across the closet rod in her tower bedroom.

How could one wear a pretty dress to cocktails and dinner unless one owned a pretty dress?

Until now she had thought she owned two: a rose-colored print and a demure white shirtdress with small pearl buttons down the front. But now they both looked hideous—like something "prissy Miss Martin" would wear. *And why not?* It was prissy Miss Martin who had picked them out!

Jan swallowed her rising panic. Perhaps she had a fever. Hot one minute and cold the next, she tried to imagine herself in the solarium of the great house sipping a drink and gazing at Tony. What on earth would she say to him? What was he thinking, now that he had kissed her?

Recalling that moment, she was sure that in his arms she had behaved like a dead fish. Yet he had kissed her again—would he have done that if he hadn't enjoyed it the first time?

She ran the tip of her tongue along her lips and told herself that if she had a fever she shouldn't go. Probably she was coming down with something. Certainly her stomach was queasy enough! But then, glancing at the clock on the dresser, she went flying into the bathroom . . . in forty minutes Tony was expecting her!

The luscious-smelling oil and the cloud of heavenly scent that rose with the steam from the tub gradually soothed her, and, feeling more assured, she allowed herself the luxury of a brief soak while she admired the vibrant colors of the flowering gloxinias, African violets, and geraniums that were banked along the tub's sides. Finally, refreshed and a fraction less nervous, she stood on the fur rug and dried herself with a velvet-piled towel, thinking how spoiled she had become in only a day's time and how difficult it would be to adjust, once she was back in Paris again, to the bath down the hall she shared with three other tenants.

When she was back in her bedroom, she saw that the excitement of the afternoon had brought a flattering pink tinge to her cheeks, and in a better frame of mind she imagined that the white dress was not so bad after all; but when she had slipped it down over her slender hips and fastened the pearl buttons, she surveyed herself with disappointment. She had thought to wear her hair loose and flowing in the hope that Tony would approve. But the girl staring back at her from the mirror looked like a ten-year-old on her way to Sunday school. *Was there still time to change into the rose print?*

She decided to chance it, but when she pulled it out of the closet and held it against her, she saw no improvement. The two outfits were equally awful.

In despair, she flung the rose print onto the bed and, leaving on the white dress, snatched up her hair and twisted it into the familiar knot at the back of her head. Briefly she considered leaving off her glasses, but before she started down the stairs she put them on again. Tony knew she couldn't see without them. Just to embarrass her he might be devil enough to invite her to read a book!

Shivering with excitement, Jan came out into the soft, airy evening and crossed the paved courtyard to the main house. The solarium where Tony had instructed her to meet him overlooked the back garden, she reminded herself, having seen it that morning on the way to the breakfast room, and she took comfort in the thought that at least she knew her way around. But once inside the house, she was overcome with fright again and stopped in the foyer.

While she hesitated, the maid who had shown her to the tower the evening before appeared and directed her down the hallway. Ahead she could see the solarium—a bright, many-windowed room filled with plants and comfortable-looking furniture upholstered in apricot and yellow—and she could see Tony standing at the bar talking to a woman.

The woman, seated on a stool beside him, wore a shimmering crepe-de-chine evening skirt and, over the voluptuous curve of her breast, a beaded, off-the-shoulder blouse. Her hand was on Tony's arm, and her flawless profile was lifted toward his face in a pose of intimate absorption.

Over her head, Tony caught sight of Jan. "Oh—so there you are," he said. Stepping around the bar, he came toward her. "Maria and I were wondering if you'd had second thoughts about coming to dinner."

Second and third and tenth *thoughts if you only knew!* she wanted to cry, but she moved into the room with a silly smile on her lips, her gaze anxiously shifting from Tony's face to the bar where the sleekly attired beauty acknowledged her entrance with a single languid glance and then turned back to her drink.

This was Maria? Numbly Jan recalled the plump dowager image that had come to mind when Tony had mentioned her name that morning. *She owns the adjoining villa,* he had said. Looking at her now, Jan swallowed. *How convenient.*

When the introductions were over, Jan took the drink Tony held out to her and gratefully let a swallow of it slide down her parched throat. She had no idea what it was. It burned like fire, and she soon set it down, but she was thankful that it took her mind away, for a moment at least, from the cold look of inspection Maria Bertani had now fixed upon her.

"You're Tony's new discovery?" Maria said at last, her cultured voice falling into the silence between them with the ease of a stone slipping into a pool. "I'd never have imagined you to be a designer."

"Jan isn't a *clothes* designer, Maria," said Tony, and then they both laughed. Jan felt her face grow scarlet, but with confident ease Tony smoothed over his remark. "Maria expects anyone who has anything at all to do with design to look as avant-garde as those Frenchmen who sell her their zany fashions."

Maria pretended annoyance. "You don't like this?" Seductively she moved slender fingers across her beaded breast. "Henri Gabon did this for me alone."

Tony smiled wryly. "I'm sure he knew if you didn't buy it, some other extravagant female would."

Maria's limpid gaze rested for a moment on Jan's imitation-pearl buttons. "Not many women, extravagant or not, could have afforded it, darling."

Finally the seemingly endless cocktail hour came to a close, but dinner, Jan found, was worse.

First came a salad of duck breasts, walnuts, and raisins, then a salmon mousse with a sour sauce, followed by saddle of lamb and ending with something Tony called a *cassis sorbet* with summer berries. Halfway through, Jan felt she might burst, though she had only nibbled at the various portions that were served her.

The conversation, centering on herself, was equally distressing. In great detail, Tony described their flight, the afternoon in Como, and their dinner meeting with Angela and Roberto Mignelli. Jan held her breath, wondering what he would say when he launched into an account of their tower luncheon; but, when Maria bent to her dessert, he only grinned wickedly and said that Jan had allowed him a brief glimpse of her latest work.

"Maria, you must have a look at it, too," he said. Then, noticing Jan's surprised expression, he added, "Oh, don't worry. It's quite all right for Maria to see anything you do."

Maria's lips curved sardonically. "I am a major stockholder in the firm and a member of the board of directors. Each Friday I go into Como and for three or four abysmally boring hours I listen while Tony and his self-important artists agonize over their pencil scratchings."

Before Jan could think of a response, Tony said with a touch of annoyance, "Those 'pencil scratchings' earn you quite a nice living."

"I would make the same nice living if I never set foot in the place again," Maria replied sharply.

Jan looked from one to the other, wondering if they were about to quarrel.

But Tony took Maria's acid remark in stride. "Nevertheless, I think you're warming up to your role. I've noticed several times lately that you've contributed to the design pool."

Maria speared a berry and popped it into her mouth. "Anything to relieve the monotony of those awful sessions. Besides"—she gave Tony an arch look—"it's good for your poor designers to have something interesting to think about now and then."

Coffee was served in the library, and afterward Jan, trying to hide her relief, excused herself.

"I'll walk with you back to the tower," said Tony, rising as she did.

"Why, Tony—" Maria's laughter mocked him. "What an old mother hen you've become. It's hardly a dozen steps to the tower. I imagine that—" Her eyebrows rose quizzically. "—Jan, is it?—can find her own way quite nicely."

Smarting at the obvious affront, Jan said, "I'm sure I can."

But Tony was not to be deterred. "I'll be back in a moment," he told Maria and steered Jan toward the door.

As they crossed the courtyard, Tony said, "You mustn't mind Maria. She breathes only rarefied air."

Still annoyed by Maria's pretense of having forgotten her name, Jan said stiffly, "I don't know what you mean."

"I mean that Maria has been treated all her life as if she were God's special gift to the universe. She's been pampered and babied and showered with every luxury. She's been educated in the finest Swiss schools, and she's traveled extensively with her grandparents—who, incidentally, were distant relatives of my own grandfather and cofounders with him in the firm. The world of commerce is so remote from Maria's experience that it is difficult for her to understand that anyone who works for a living is a flesh-and-blood creature the same as herself."

"I didn't notice that she tried very hard," answered Jan.

Tony halted and, turning her around in the shadow of the tower, said firmly, "Perhaps Maria and I were rude tonight. We have known each other since childhood, and we often forget that the little jokes we share sometimes have an abrasive effect on those who don't know us well. If that happened this evening, I'm sorry."

Jan was trembling, but she answered crisply, "You needn't apologize. I'm not nearly so thin-skinned as you seem to think."

Her spirited reference to his remark of the evening before seemed to amuse him, and he said with a smile, "That's good news. Very good news indeed." The smile broadened. "Perhaps some progress was made this afternoon, after all."

Jan held her breath. *Did he mean to kiss her?*

But to her disappointment he reached around her and opened the tower door. Light spilled across the stones and framed them in its glow. Tony said casually, "I noticed you were interested in my books tonight. Feel free, if you wish, to make use of the library."

"Won't I disturb you?" she said stiffly, fighting the urge to be taken into his arms.

He shrugged. "Hardly. I won't be here."

"But you said you'd be in and out!"

Her response had come too quickly, and Tony's gaze hardened, making it plain that he had caught the distress in her voice.

"I'll be mostly out, I'm afraid," he said evenly. "Generally I can get away only for the weekends."

"Oh." She forced herself to speak casually. "Then you'll be leaving tomorrow."

He nodded. "Quite early, in fact. So I'll say good night."

Jan watched him go and then hurried up the winding stairs. She undressed quickly in the dark and then stationed herself by the windowsill, her eyes trained on the lighted entrance of the great house for Maria's departure.

By midnight the entire house was dark, but if Maria Bertani left to go back to her own villa, she went another way.

Chapter Seven

For several days after Tony had returned to Como, Jan spent most of her time in the tower working and reading and staring for long stretches out the windows at the lush countryside that surrounded the villa. The first day she took her meals in the main house, but she felt strange and out of place sitting alone at the long table in the dining room. After that she asked that whatever was being prepared for the staff be sent over to the tower, and she found eating alone there much more to her liking.

But toward the end of the week even the atmosphere in the tower, as comfortable and cozy as it was, began to pall. Early on Thursday morning she put on a shirt and a pair of faded jeans, tied a scarf around her head, and set off with her sketchbook in a postdawn mist for a tramp through the woods.

To her delight she discovered carefully marked

trails leading in all directions through the tangled masses of greenery that she had viewed previously only from above. The paths were like sun-speckled tunnels, and frequently she paused, kneeling in the soft earth to sketch a butterfly or a flower or a spiraling tendril of fern.

Several hours passed before she finally emerged from the undergrowth, and she was surprised to find herself at the top of a series of wide marble steps that led down into the waters of Lake Como. The tip of the promontory which Tony had spoken of as Bellagio's greatest attraction was visible on the left. On the opposite side of the lake the mountains were footed on the shore. Tucked into their hollows were countless red-roofed villas.

Breathless with the beauty of the place, Jan sat down on the top step and stared dreamily about her. But after a minute or two her gaze came full circle, and she was surprised to see that she was not alone. Eyeing her from a wind-protected nook toward the bottom of the steps was Maria Bertani. Narrow strips of swimsuit cloth covered the strategic points of her svelte body, and one hand was raised against the morning sun for a clearer view of Jan.

For a minute they stared at each other. Then, in a few effortless strides, Maria climbed toward her. "Have you come to swim?"

Noting the annoyed look on Maria's face, Jan was glad she had not. "I've been sketching in the woods. I had no idea the water was so near."

"All the best villas front the water," said Maria loftily. Then, with a pointed look at the wide expanse of marble, she added, "This happens to be part of mine."

"Oh!" Jan stood up. "I've trespassed, then, haven't I? I'm sorry. I followed the paths from the Villa Torelli. I supposed I was still on that property."

"Tony and I share this bathing spot. It's quite deep and suitable only for experienced swimmers."

A shiver rippled up Jan's spine. "Which I am not," she said. "Thanks for warning me. I think I'll stick to the pool."

"Sit down," said Maria abruptly. "I'll have a look at your sketches."

Jan's fingers tightened on the cardboard cover of her sketchbook. "These are only rough drawings."

A sardonic twist curled Maria's scarlet mouth. "Everything you people do could be described that way as far as I'm concerned."

"The work I saw in the showrooms in Como was excellent, I thought," said Jan, trying to cover her annoyance with a polite smile. "Certainly Torelli Silks has the reputation of turning out only the best."

"My—what a loyal fan you are." Maria surveyed her coldly. "Tony must be quite pleased with your attitude. Or is that why you've adopted it? To please him?"

Jan stiffened. "I've been an admirer of Torelli Silks for quite a long time."

"Oh? Do you buy them?"

Jan flushed. "I've read about them."

Maria fingered the edge of her swimsuit bra and

smiled disdainfully. "It isn't quite the same thing, is it?"

Jan had had enough. "I'm sure I don't know. If you'll excuse me, I'll get on with my walk. I'm sorry I disturbed you."

"Don't go." It was more a command than a request. Reluctantly Jan halted. Maria reminded her, "I haven't seen your sketches."

"I doubt if you'd be interested in them. If the sessions in Como bore you, I'm sure my work would, too."

"I shall be the judge of that," Maria said and put out her hand for the sketchpad. Jan was on the point of refusing, but just in time she remembered Tony's remark that Maria was entitled to see whatever she did, and reluctantly she handed over the tablet.

Together they sat down on the marble steps, and while Maria leafed languidly through her book, Jan took advantage of the opportunity to study the other woman. She had never seen anyone so fascinatingly flawless. Obviously Maria had been swimming, but not a hair of her carefully coiffed tresses was out of place.

Is that how Tony thinks I should look? Jan stared intently at the intricately woven coronet of Maria's rich black hair and tried without success to imagine such towering elaborateness atop her own head. Jan's face was broad at the brow and narrow at the chin, but Maria's was a perfect oval. Her green eyes were widely spaced and her nose delicately straight. As far as Jan could see, there was not a single blemish on her ivory complexion. Her lips were perfectly painted, as were her tapering fingernails, and the lines of her body were as perfect as the rest of her.

Maria interrupted her perusal in a voice sharp with annoyance. "What are you staring at?"

Jan met her angry gaze and flushed. "I beg your pardon. I was admiring your hair."

"Really? I shouldn't have thought glamor would appeal to you."

"It doesn't," said Jan flatly. "But you're well suited to it."

Maria's green eyes flashed fire. "Then I must tell Paul when I go to the salon this afternoon that I want my hair restyled. I won't have it typecasting me."

Jan stood up. "May I have my sketchbook, please?"

"You may when I'm finished with it." Maria ran a fingernail disdainfully over the edge of the pages." "What shall I tell Tony you've been doing when I go to Como tomorrow for my weekly drudge?"

"Tell him I've been working."

Maria cast a scornful look at the tablet. "If I'm to make myself convincing, then I shall have to accompany you back to the villa and see what you have there. I certainly can't tell anything from this."

The remark shattered what remained of Jan's control. "Why do you bother to go to the design meetings if you find them so distasteful?"

"That's really not your affair, is it?" said Maria icily. Then a superior smile curled her lips. "However, I don't mind telling you. I go because Tony has the idea that a wife should know as much about the family business as her husband." Amused, she watched the color drain out of Jan's face. "Isn't that quaint?"

Jan swallowed. "You and Tony are to be married?"

"Eventually. Does that surprise you?"

"Not really." Jan held her pencil-smudged fingers tightly together before her. "I hadn't thought of it one way or the other."

"No?" Maria eyed her shrewdly. "Then I'm glad I mentioned it. Tony is an attractive man, as I'm sure you've noticed. Occasionally, some silly girl at the mill or one of the clerks in the showroom is taken with him. It's always so unpleasant when we have to let her go."

Jan turned away. "I need to get back."

"I'll walk along with you." Maria pulled a short striped robe over her swimsuit and fell into step beside her. "It will soon be lunchtime. I'll have the cook at Villa Torelli fix us one of her divine shrimp salads, and you can show me your work." She yawned lazily. "I may even have a nap in your ivory tower before I go to the hairdresser." Her look was openly challenging. "What would you say to that?"

Jan quickened her pace. "Do as you please."

Maria, however, did not take a nap in the tower, nor did she stay for lunch. After a short time spent looking over Jan's work, she suddenly pleaded a headache and made a hasty departure. With relief Jan watched from the upper-story windows as she moved off through the trees, still clad in her bikini and robe.

Jan lunched alone on an airy vol-au-vent sent over

76

from the main kitchen and had just settled down to work when an impatient honking shattered the afternoon quiet. When the noise continued, Jan went to the window and discovered that the source of the disturbance was a bright yellow car parked at her own doorstep. Hurrying down the stairs, she saw to her dismay that it was Maria, dressed now in a cream-colored suit and silk blouse in shades of peacock blue and magenta.

"Drive with me into Bellagio," she commanded as soon as Jan stepped out into the sunlight. "I've decided to go on to Como today after I've had my hair done, and you can bring my car back when you've dropped me off at the salon."

Jan stared at her. At least four men were employed at the Villa Torelli, and certainly Maria had her own share of employees—any one of whom could chauffeur her about.

"I'm working," she said flatly.

"Get in, please," Maria said imperiously. "Ignacio is due to pick me up in Tony's Rolls at four o'clock, and I want to be in Como by dinnertime."

"You'll have to find someone else to drive you, then," said Jan curtly. "I'm in the middle of something."

Maria's ripe lips tightened. "If someone else had been available, I should certainly never have resorted to you. This is a festival day. All the servants will be in church until the middle of the afternoon."

From where Jan stood, she could see a young boy chopping in the kitchen garden, but realizing the futility of further objections, she climbed into the front seat beside Maria. *Anyway,* she consoled herself, *what was twenty minutes more or less? She could spend that much time arguing.*

"What kind of festival is it?" she said to Maria.

"How should I know?" the other girl replied. "Something to do with the vines, probably. These people observe so many ridiculous customs it's impossible to keep up with them, even if one cared to."

The rest of the way they drove in silence. Apparently, thought Jan, Maria considered herself so far above those who waited upon her that she did not even associate her own nationality with theirs. How could Tony find a woman with such an exalted opinion of herself interesting enough to marry?

To her discomfort, the question struck the vulnerable spot she had avoided examining since morning when Maria had announced that she and Tony would one day be married. But forced to think of it now, Jan admitted that there was a logic to the plan. She knew that Europeans often married in order to combine fortunes, and since Maria's wealth was grounded in Torelli Silks—as was Tony's—marriage probably seemed to them the natural step to take, whether they loved each other or not.

It disturbed Jan to think of Tony's entering a marriage without love, and she shut out the thought by concentrating on the beauty of the blue-and-gold day. When in a few moments Maria turned down a tree-lined street near the center of Bellagio and drew up before the hairdresser's salon, she felt an enormous relief. The trip had taken less time than she'd feared. With any luck at all, she could be back at her drawing table in five minutes or so.

"Where shall I leave your car?" she said as Maria got out.

"At the Villa Torelli. My maid, Ann Janell, will call for it later. But before you leave town, step into that shop across the way—Jean LeCou's—you can see the sign. I had a dress fitted there last week, and I want it picked up."

Jan, still in her jeans, bristled. "I'm not dressed to go into a shop."

"Oh, don't be silly," scoffed Maria. "It's not as if you were a customer."

"That's beside the point."

"The *point* is that I want the dress picked up, and I want it picked up today," said Maria in a hard tone. "It won't take a minute. Why are you making such a fuss?"

Jan gritted her teeth. "Is there anything else I can do for you?"

"Yes, as a matter of fact. You can fill the car with petrol." Maria's lip curled. "Unless you do, you probably won't make it back to the villa."

The name of the shop was arranged in filigreed letters on a sign beside the door, which a uniformed attendant opened for Jan. Once inside the perfumed interior she was greeted with raised eyebrows until she announced what she had come for. Then the salesgirl, evidently mistaking her for an American guest of Maria's, invited her to look around while she waited.

Everything was frightfully expensive, as Jan had anticipated, but uncommonly beautiful also. In a few minutes she had lost all track of time browsing among the racks of tempting ensembles. There were shiny, lustrous chintzes and piques, sports clothes in unfamiliar glazed fabrics, and quilted poplins for casual wear. For evening there was one whole wall of frothy creations that would turn the head of any girl, but one in particular caught Jan's eye—a red silk organza that stood out from all the rest in its elegance.

Jan stood gazing at it with naked longing until the salesgirl, returning with Maria's purchase, caught her look and invited her to try it on.

Jan blinked. The thought had not occurred to her, but why not? Maria's interruption had spoiled her taste for work, and it might be fun, just for a lark, to pretend—even for a little while—that she was rich enough to afford clothes like those Maria wore. "Yes," she said, turning toward the salesgirl. "I would like to slip it on."

In the dressing room, Jan stood still while the girl fussed over every detail, arranging the dropped waist of the gown first and then the flowing skirt. But when she stood back, both she and Jan stared in amazement at the transformation the dress had made in Jan's appearance.

"Ohh . . ." the girl breathed in delight. "Signorina—it was made for you."

Jan had to agree. With her hair hidden beneath the scarf, her strong cheekbones came to the fore, lending her chin and the hollows of her cheeks a delicate softness she had never observed in her face before. Even her wide mouth, picking up the glow of the dress, appeared appealingly sensuous. Her waist seemed narrower, her bust fuller.

A shiver of pleasure rippled over her. *If one simple gown could make such a difference . . . !* Jan caught her breath. Then she heard her own voice come back at her as if it were a stranger's. "Bring some other things, please. That Mandarin-style print in the desert tones, for one—and a swimsuit, perhaps. I'd like that in blue."

The girl hurried away.

An hour and a half later, Jan emerged from the shop accompanied by the uniformed attendant carrying an armful of boxes—only one of which belonged to Maria.

Everything she had bought would have to come back tomorrow, she thought dizzily as she drove away. *She had gone crazy in there!* But what fun it had been! Aunt Elizabeth would rise up from her grave if she knew how much money would have to be exchanged for the contents of those shiny white boxes on the seat beside her. The red organza alone would cost three-fourths of her first paycheck, to say nothing of the other things—the Mandarin print . . . the button-front overalls in ivory shantung. *Heaven knew where she would ever wear those!* She had bought a pencil-slim dress suit in madras, too, with a wrap jacket and pants to match, and who could have resisted that slinky swimsuit?

It was a wardrobe for a queen—but even a queen might have difficulty paying for it! The thing to do was to go straight back to the shop and explain that the whole spending spree had been a mistake and that the account she had opened must be closed at once. At least then she could get a good night's sleep.

It was a prudent impulse, and she might have followed through on it, but just as she came into the paved courtyard where she could have turned around, she saw a sullen-looking girl positioned with her hands on her hips in front of the tower door.

Jan's blood froze. *Ann Janell!* She had completely forgotten about her.

Slamming on the brakes, Jan slid out of the car with Maria's package. "I'm so sorry to be late," she said breathlessly. "Have you been waiting long?"

The girl reached for the box and swiftly stuffed it into a shopping bag she took up from the ground. "Only five minutes." She stared warily at Jan and blinked her large, cowlike eyes. *"Two* minutes. I don't go anywhere. I stand here and wait."

The girl seemed so benumbed that Jan hesitated to turn over the car keys. "Is the festival over?"

The girl frowned.

"I go now, signorina." She started past Jan, who remembered her own packages suddenly and made haste to get them out of the car before Ann Janell, her patience at an end, whipped off across the driveway.

Climbing the stairs, Jan wondered at Maria's choice of maids. Surely there was available in this lovely Lombardian valley a servant with a sunnier disposition than Ann Janell's! Then, remembering Maria's own acid temperament, she shrugged, deciding that they were well suited to each other, after all.

Finding work out of the question after her spending spree, Jan got out of her jeans and wrinkled shirt and drew a bath, noting with pleasure as she did so that fresh plants had been substituted for those that had stopped blooming, and that an additional array of perfumes and oils, as well as a fresh supply of towels—this time of palest yellow—had been left for her by the cleaning maid.

For half an hour she luxuriated in the warm, fragrant water, and then, wrapping herself in the largest of the towels, she went back to the bedroom to re-examine her finery. Before she was done, she had tried on every stitch again and pirouetted before the mirror at least a dozen times.

There was not one purchase she would willingly give up, she mused later over dinner. But they would all have to go. When she returned to Paris there were sure to be lean times. She must save her money.

But the thought of leaving the Villa Torelli opened a hollow place inside her. Her trial period was not yet up, but already she felt more at home here than in any place she had ever been. If her work was satisfactory to Tony, then she was determined to stay as long as she could.

Briefly she wondered how in this remote corner of the world a Plains girl, born and bred to the most meager of circumstances, could have accustomed herself so easily to the opulent style of life that Tony accepted as a matter of course. *It would not even be difficult,* she thought as her fancy took wing, *to imagine herself as mistress here, planning sumptuous banquets . . . wearing gorgeous clothes . . . and— most of all—loving Tony.*

Restlessly she pushed back from the table.

Dreams like those could lead nowhere but to pain and misery. Tony belonged to Maria. The sooner she accepted that, the easier it would be to say goodbye when the time came.

Deciding that a walk was what was needed to clear her head of nonsense, she set out briskly in the direction of the tennis court. It was the first time she had made a close inspection of the grounds, and she discovered, besides the swimming pool and the tennis court, a riding stable, an elaborate greenhouse—the source, no doubt, of the plants in her bathroom—and a dog kennel.

The Borzoi, Napoleon, was there, and he greeted her with a series of welcoming barks, though they had seen each other only once. Kneeling beside the wire enclosure, Jan stroked the long, moist nose of the beautiful animal, aware suddenly that she herself was as lonely as he.

"I wish I could take you out for a stroll, my friend," she commiserated, and Nappy's eager whine indicated that he shared her desire.

After a few minutes, Jan said goodbye to the dog, but she resolved at the first opportunity to ask Tony's permission to take Nappy with her whenever she went walking.

When would she have that opportunity? she wondered, climbing the stairs toward her bedroom. Would Tony return to the villa tomorrow night as he had done the previous Friday? Or had he come then only because he was delivering her? Maria was in Como tonight, she remembered with a heavy heart. Probably at this moment she and Tony were sharing dinner—or perhaps they were in each other's arms.

Depressed by the picture her imagination provided, she retired early, hoping to lose herself in a book she had tucked away in her suitcase, but before she had read many pages, her thoughts strayed again to Tony and Maria.

Already they were lovers. That was obvious, and she would be wise to face the fact. She would do well to realize, too, that they were special people. They lived exotic lives that she could never hope to share—though she had tried to today, she thought ruefully. That was what had been at the bottom of her reckless spending spree—the desire to know what it felt like to be the kind of woman Tony Torelli might fall in love with.

With a sigh, she leaned over and turned out the light. *She had found out what it felt like,* she thought, lying back in the darkness. She had found out, and she liked it. She liked it far too much for her own good.

Chapter Eight

The day after her shopping spree in Bellagio, Jan found herself at odds with everything. She got up late, thinking that she would go back to Jean LeCou's at once with the clothes she had bought but not paid for. Then she realized that, aside from walking, she had no way to get there. The chauffeured Rolls-Royce—even if she could have worked up the nerve to ask for it—had taken Maria to Como. Ann Janell had Maria's car, and as far as Jan knew, no other transportation was available.

For a time she toyed with the idea of inquiring of the cook whether there were some other way to get into Bellagio, but she delayed with one excuse or another and finally convinced herself that it might be a better tactic to wait one more day to return her purchases. By that time she might have worked up the courage to simply announce to the clerk that she had changed her mind.

The issue of the clothes temporarily resolved, she decided to sketch and halfheartedly poked around in the studio searching for her design book, which oddly enough she seemed to have misplaced. *By Freudian impulse,* she told herself wryly when the book was nowhere to be found. She had no real desire to work, and her subconscious, aware of that, had evidently blinded her to its whereabouts.

In that case, she decided, *she would read.*

But her book held no more interest for her in the morning light than it had the evening before, and she soon cast it aside in favor of going for a swim. However, when she hauled out her old swimsuit from the bureau drawer, it appeared even more drab and unappealing than she had remembered, and she tossed it aside feeling more disgruntled than ever.

Of course there was the new swimsuit . . .

Lovingly, her hands moved over its silken softness in the drawer. Such an expensive bit of fluff! But she didn't dare get it wet—not unless she meant to keep it.

Despite Jan's resistance, the idea grew. *Why not keep it?* Surely she should be allowed one indulgence at least, one souvenir of her Italian escapade.

In a moment the reckless side of her nature took over. For the first time in her life she was earning an enormous salary, she told herself. She deserved to spend some of it foolishly. After all, she was taking back the other things she had bought. She should have some small reward for that act of prudence.

In less time than it took her to marshal another

argument, she had wriggled into the suit and stood gazing with renewed pleasure at herself in the mirror. Like the red organza, the swimsuit seemed to transform her into a glamorous stranger—one she couldn't stop admiring. The skillfully cut cloth hugged the trim lines of her hips like skin and molded itself, even as scandalously brief as it was, to the seductive swell of her firm young breasts.

Dizzy with delight at the picture she presented, Jan swept up her hair in a careless swirl atop her head and, tossing aside her heavy glasses, fished around in the drawer until she came up with an outlandish pair of sunshades a fellow student in Paris had given her in gratitude for assistance with a sketching project.

Fixing the sunglasses on her nose, Jan pranced off toward the pool, reveling in the fantasy of what it would be like to be mistress of the Villa Torelli, an intoxicating illusion that stayed with her throughout the remainder of the morning and was reinforced at one o'clock when an elaborate lunch was served to her beside the cabana.

Afterward she visited for a time with Nappy, poking a few luncheon delicacies through the wire fence at him and giggling delightedly when he laid his grateful muzzle against her fingers and gazed at her with his soulful brown eyes.

Finally, at three, worn out with the pleasures of the day, she stretched out beside the pool and was soon fast asleep.

Shortly after four, Tony arrived back at the villa from Como. Passing the pool on his way to give

Nappy a quick greeting before he changed from his city attire into something more comfortable, he was startled to see a slender stranger, her face blocked by a pair of enormous sunglasses, sound asleep on the tile coping of his swimming pool.

Drawing near, he intended a closer look, but Nappy, catching sight of him, set up a fearful ruckus.

At once Jan awoke. At first she was too dazed to realize where she was, but when she lifted off her sunglasses and her glance fell on Tony staring incredulously, she sprang to her feet, hands instinctively flying toward the scanty top of her swimsuit. "Tony!" she gasped. "What are *you* doing here?"

"I'm looking at you." His appreciative gaze slid up her body. "What's your excuse?"

Pulling at the skimpy suit, she sputtered, "I haven't spent all my time since you left lying around the pool, if that's what you're thinking."

"Lord," he murmured with a sardonic twist to his sensuous lips. "It's prissy Miss Martin again, lurking in that lovely frame. Are we never to be rid of her?" Then, in answer to Jan's angry look, he added languidly, "It's selfish of you, you know, to keep a stunning figure hidden inside that baggy linen skirt and jacket you're always wearing everywhere."

"I haven't *been* everywhere," she answered hotly, not yet able to believe that he had caught her so nearly naked. "Besides, a linen suit is quite appropriate for a plane ride."

"Yes, Aunt Elizabeth." His eyes glittered. "And a white nightgown is nice for dinner, too."

Her face turned scarlet at this tardy reference to

the pristine garb she had worn to the great house. "I don't need you to tell me how to dress."

"Perhaps you do—except when it comes to swim-suits," he replied. "Incidentally," he said as a devilish grin spread over his face, "is that one made for getting wet?"

"Tony!" she screeched when she saw his arm come out, but it was too late. He had already given her a light shove. Gasping with astonishment, Jan toppled over into the water. In a moment she bobbed up, spluttering and splashing.

But just as quickly she sank again.

Abruptly Tony's laughter stopped. "Jan?" He leaned over the edge of the pool. "Jan!" he cried out. In an instant he had dived into the water and was beside her, snatching at her flailing arms, then going under himself as she began climbing his shoulders. They floundered together, Jan clutching wildly at his neck and grasping a handful of hair while he struggled toward the ladder leading up to safety. But at last he was able to drag them both over the side, where Jan finally let go and sprawled limply in a spreading circle of water.

"Good *heavens!*" White-faced and more relieved to have her out of the water then he cared to show, Tony shook off his sodden suit coat. "Why didn't you say you couldn't swim?"

"Why didn't you ask"—she choked—"before you tried to drown me?"

"I rescued you!"

"That wouldn't have been necessary if you hadn't been so brainless and pushed me in in the first place."

"You got what you asked for." Grim-faced, he poured water out of one shoe. "If you intend to go on lounging around swimming pools, I'd advise you to have a sign made warning people that you're there only for decoration."

"I can swim!" she answered indignantly. "But when I'm shoved, I go in with my mouth open."

"I'll say you do!"

They glared at each other. Then, suddenly, Jan giggled. "You should see yourself."

"You think I'm funny-looking, do you? My favorite suit ruined, my shoes shrinking by the minute—" Grabbing hold of her again, he made as if to toss her back into the pool, but she screamed and threw her arms around his neck.

For a moment they struggled. Then they were still, clinging wetly to each other. "You impossible wench," he muttered thickly.

Jan's breath came out a ragged whisper. "Let me go. You're wet as a mackerel."

"Am I really?" he said. Then his mouth came down. He kissed her, the damp, vibrant column of his body molding itself to hers with a fierce intensity that took her breath away. An electric thrill shot through her, and in a surge of unexpected joy she yielded her lips to his, tensing against the hard thrust of his thighs as prickles of passion spiraled through her nerve centers.

"You're delicious wet," he muttered, nibbling at her earlobe, then sending his lips back to the hollow of her throat and up again to her mouth.

Shaken by the erotic tremors that swept over her, Jan pulled away.

"Come inside," he said hoarsely.

"No—I don't want to." Her heart leaped to her throat. "I'm not through sunbathing."

"The hell you aren't," he answered and swooped her up into his arms. He carried her, struggling—but only halfheartedly—across the paved courtyard.

"Put me down!" she begged breathlessly. "What will the servants say?"

"Do you think I give a damn?"

"*I* do!"

"I don't give a damn about that, either."

With her still in his arms, he mounted the tower stairs. But when he had her in her bedroom, he set her down without ceremony, dripping on the golden carpet, and strode into the bathroom. She stood where she was, eyes wide, listening to the rush of water come into the tub.

"There," he said, re-entering the bedroom. "There's a body of water you'll be safe in."

"I didn't ask you to draw me a bath!"

Disregarding her temper, he strolled to the doorway. "We're having dinner in Bellagio. Be downstairs in your sitting room in an hour."

"You tyrant!" Jan glared. "What if I'm not?"

He turned. His eyes swept over her shivering body. "Then I'll come up and drag the tub."

The restaurant to which Tony took Jan was on the opposite side of the promontory from the villa.

"La Punta Spartivento," he announced when they were seated in the twilight on a terrace above the cerulean waters of Lake Como. "What do you think of it?"

"It's beautiful," she murmured, feeling as if she were in a dream.

His glance slid lazily over her slender lines, flatteringly accented by the ivory shantung overalls that at the last minute she had dared to wear. "It's no more beautiful than you," he murmured, eyeing her with appreciation. "I take back every word I said this afternoon."

She gave him a startled look. "Every word?"

Her disappointed tone amused him. "At least what I said about your clothes. Nothing from Aunt Elizabeth's trunk tonight. You look stunning."

Uneasily she dropped her gaze. What she had secretly longed for had happened. He was intrigued by her—and she had no idea how to handle him!

"You've shown me a side of you today I'd never seen before," he went on, reaching for her hand. "Would that have happened if I hadn't caught you unawares—just being yourself?"

Jan dodged his question. "I didn't know that you were coming to the villa today."

"That's not what I asked."

She looked across the blue water. "All right, then. Probably if I had known you were coming I wouldn't have been by the pool, no." She flushed. "And I certainly would have been wearing something else."

"Why?" He studied her. "Why do you hide behind those awful glasses and that wretched little knot of hair?" His fingertips smoothed her wrists. "Thank God you've left them both behind tonight."

"I'm not hiding."

"I think you are."

"Aunt Elizabeth believed—" She paused, shifting

her emphasis away from the aunt he so frequently mocked. "I was reared to be seen and not heard—and not even seen unless it was absolutely necessary. I become uncomfortable when I'm pushed to the foreground."

He gave her a sardonic smile. "At least if one remains in the background the likelihood of being pushed into the middle of a swimming pool is lessened, is it not?"

She looked back at him. "Why did you throw me in?"

He shrugged. "Impulse."

"Simply because it occurred to you? Is that why you did it?"

"Something like that."

She withdrew her hands from his and put them in her lap. "I've never known anyone like you."

"Nor I you," he answered quietly.

"Everything I do is practical and purposeful except—"

He peered intently at her. "Except what?"

She had been on the verge of confiding in him about the reckless feelings that sometimes invaded her and resulted in the daydreams from which her most successful designs were drawn. As close as she felt to him at this moment, she was still too uncertain of his feelings for her to share with him the intimate thoughts concerning her work. "Except for something silly and impulsive that I did yesterday," she substituted quickly. "I can't imagine what got into me."

Looking at her flushed face, his gaze sharpened,

and his eyes took on a luminous, compelling quality. "Tell me about it."

"You'll laugh. It's so stupid." But she found herself wanting to tell him and recounted with an excited flush how she had gone into the dress shop merely to pick up a package and come out with an armload of expensive clothes. "As yet unpaid for," she finished ruefully.

The tale delighted him. "Is this one of your purchases?" he inquired, fingering the collar of the shantung overalls.

She nodded. "The swimsuit was another."

"Bravo for you!" Tony lifted his wineglass. "Here's to many more shopping expeditions. Tell me—how did you happen into that swanky shop in the first place? Have you been sneaking into town every day, licking your chops over what their windows had to offer?"

Jan shook her head. "I was on an errand for Maria."

He frowned. "Maria is sending you on errands?"

"Only this once," Jan explained and then went on to tell him how she had met Maria at the lake and what had happened afterward. She was careful to leave out any hint of criticism of Maria's demanding behavior, but she saw when she was finished that Tony was annoyed anyway.

He said with another frown, "Maria was on her way to Como when you left her?"

"Yes." Jan was sorry she had introduced Maria into the conversation, but there was no shutting her out now. "Your chauffeur was to meet her at the hairdresser's, she said. She told me she intended to report to you concerning my work." Jan hesitated. "Did she?"

"No," he answered abruptly. "I didn't see her. Something came up and she went to Venice instead." Then, to Jan's relief, his dark expression lifted and he inquired in a pleasanter tone, "Why don't you tell me about your work yourself? How is it going?"

She felt shy again. "It's going very well."

Their meal was served then, bringing to a halt any further discussion as they admired the elaborate chicken concoction baked in clay that had been molded in the form of a duck. This, accompanied by fresh vegetables, fruit, cheese, and a clear red wine Tony called Barolo Pio Cesare, created an altogether delightful repast that left Jan feeling relaxed and comfortable again.

It wasn't until they were once more on the road driving toward the villa that Tony reintroduced the subject of her drawings.

"So you've really been working this week?"

The skepticism in his question struck Jan as oddly annoying. "Of course. I have a sketchbook full of designs." She lifted her chin defiantly. "Some of them are quite good, I think."

His mood had changed since dinner, she noticed, and now he was entirely the businessman, as he had been the first day she met him.

Keeping his eyes on the road, he said, "Do you have as many as a dozen I can take when I return to Como?"

She deserved to boast a little, she thought. "I have at least twice that many."

"I'm talking about designs that are polished enough to submit to the review board," he said curtly.

Her mouth tightened. "So am I."

"Well, then . . ." At least *that* seemed to please him. "In a week or so we should probably have some of your things on the market."

Her heart came up in her throat. "So soon? What if I'm not ready?"

"You said you thought your work was quite good."

"Well, of course, some of the designs are better than others—"

"Is it good or not?" he said sharply.

"I'll have a dozen designs ready for you tomorrow afternoon," she responded tersely.

He relaxed suddenly. "I won't need them until Monday. I'm staying over. I'm taking you with me to Premana tomorrow."

"Premana?" *Why should he do that?*

"You've read about it, of course," he said in a voice tinged with sarcasm.

His tone ruffled her. "Premana is a steelworkers' village in the mountains, I believe, famous for surgical knives and ice axes and those foot-wide cowbells the Swiss use."

"You've read about those, too, I suppose."

Inwardly she was squirming like an insect impaled upon a pin. "I imagine everyone has."

He snorted. "I doubt if Maria has—or any of the other women I know."

Now Jan was annoyed. "I don't see why not. It's right on their doorstep!"

"Maria isn't interested in things of that sort," he said tightly. Then he glanced across at Jan with a challenging look. "She and her friends lead interesting lives of their own. They see no need to look between the covers of books for their experiences."

Angry tears stung at Jan's eyes. How unfair! Of course Maria's life was full and exciting, but if she cared nothing for the marvels of her own country, what *did* she care about? "She's more self-centered than I thought," said Jan primly.

Tony snapped back at her. "Maria places no importance on such things."

"Well, *I* do!" With a haughty lift of her chin Jan folded her arms across her chest. "And I shall be happy to go to Premana and to see everything I've read about."

"And I shall be happy to take you"—he gave her a dark look—"*Miss Martin.*"

Chapter Nine

Tony called for Jan the next morning in a jeep, and when she climbed in beside him, noticing the close-fitting denims he wore and the suede vest that swung loosely away from his muscular frame, she thought with a thrill of pleasure how well suited he was to the casual look of a mountain man. He had warned her when they parted at the tower door the evening before that it would be a rugged trip and to dress accordingly.

"I'll wear my linen suit, then," she said lightly, hoping that he might interpret her teasing suggestion as a way of saying she was sorry they had quarreled, but he had only frowned and said curtly, "Pants would be more appropriate."

She had left him then and gone to bed, but she slept little, partly because she regretted that their evening, which had begun with so much promise, had ended on a sour note, and partly because her head was swarming with confused thoughts.

Tony could be so charming—and so coldly disagreeable. But she had herself to blame for his shift in mood, she reasoned, tossing restlessly on the linen sheets. It was her mention of Maria, she realized, that had spoiled the evening. Plainly, Tony was upset that Maria had not come to Como as planned. She had not returned to Bellagio for the weekend either, Jan mused and wondered what was so important in Venice that it would keep Maria away from Tony, particularly since she seemed so jealous of his attentions.

Jan's heart—where she imagined her damaged pride resided—ached as she considered the likelihood that Tony would not have kissed her or taken her to dinner if Maria had been available. Perhaps even his shoving her into the pool had been a way of expressing regret that it was she and not Maria whom he had discovered lounging there.

Her cheeks burning in the darkness, Jan had considered turning on the light and reading for a while or even going up to the studio to sketch. Anything had seemed better than restless tossing and turning.

But her troubled thoughts would not let her go. She was sensitive enough to other people's feelings to be certain that at the beginning of the evening Tony had been genuinely pleased that she was with him, and certainly he had made it plain that for once he approved of the way she looked.

She had worn her hair in a soft, shiny coil that covered one ear, and he had looked at it admiringly when he helped her from the car at the restaurant. The decision to wear the shantung outfit had been a wise one, too, though she dared not think how long it would take her to pay for it. If only she had had sense enough to keep Maria out of their conversation, they might have had a night to remember joyously instead of one that had seen them both angry.

Staring wide-eyed at the shadowy forms of the bedroom furniture, Jan wondered if perhaps Tony had felt guilty dining with another woman when Maria was the one he cared for.

But she quickly dismissed that idea. Tony had absolute confidence in himself and his decisions. Guilt played no part in his makeup. He did what he chose and felt utterly justified. *It was a pity,* she thought with a twinge of bitterness, *that he couldn't accord the same privilege to others!*

Why should he object so strenuously whenever she spoke knowledgeably about a subject? Maria seemed intelligent enough, so surely it wasn't that he admired stupid women. But whatever the reason, she had promised herself as she drifted off to sleep at last, the next day in Premana she would let him lead the way entirely. . . .

Now, however, bumping along beside Tony on the narrow road he had turned onto after they left the Strada Regina, she wondered at the wisdom of that promise. The trail they were following was perilously narrow and steep, though it had begun innocently enough with terraced vineyards and hayfields. She knew from her reading that Premana was perched high up in the mountains, but she had no way of knowing that access to it would be quite so forbidding.

"It's not much farther, is it?" she ventured timidly when they came to one particularly treacherous curve and missed by an inch scraping fenders with another vehicle on the way down.

"Only a few miles," Tony responded cheerfully. "Straight up!"

She had been wondering uneasily if he might not have chosen this backward approach to the village simply to show her that there were some things not mentioned in books, but the lightheartedness of his tone seemed to belie that he was engaged in anything vengeful and she relaxed a little, turning her attention to the spectacular views the heights afforded. She needed a holiday, she told herself, and if Tony had forgotten, as it seemed he had, that they had parted on less than pleasant terms the evening before, she was determined to enjoy whatever the day had to offer.

Waiting to speak again until they were nearly on the outskirts of the village, she cocked her head and said of a strangely melodious sound coming down off the mountain, "Church bells? There must be hundreds of them!"

Tony smiled. "What you are hearing are hammers on anvils. The forges in Premana are in use even on Saturday mornings."

Jan brought her hands together excitedly. "I can't

wait to see everything! Do you come up here often?"

"Two or three times a season. Usually when I'm looking for a smith to come down to Como and make replacement parts for our equipment. But I've grown to know a few families well, and sometimes I am invited up for special occasions."

"I see." Then a mild exclamation escaped her. "Why, look at all the hotels!" While they were talking the village had come into view, and Jan, spotting a cluster of five- and six-story buildings rising in its center, had felt a sudden shock of disappointment. "Premana isn't a tourist town, is it?"

"Far from it," Tony assured her. "What you're seeing aren't hotels—they're family dwellings. The factories are family-owned industries—as I'm sure you've read," he added with a wry grin. "The foundry is on the ground floor, the mother and father occupy the next level, and in the succeeding levels the married sons and their families live."

Nothing Jan had read had explained *that,* and she strained forward eagerly for a closer view of the narrow stone buildings stretching toward the sky. The idea had a peculiar appeal for her. Growing up alone in Aunt Elizabeth's rambling old house, she had often wished for the company of a large family. "Will we be allowed to see inside one of those?"

"If we're in luck. This one, in fact." Tony braked the car and wheeled into the front yard of a building on their right. "Bruno Viotto lives here. He's something of an unofficial mayor, and if his wife

Claretta is in her kitchen, she'll probably have a fresh batch of 'hurry-up' bread baking on the hearth." He swung his muscular frame over the side of the jeep. "Come along, we'll see."

They went first into the foundry on the ground floor where Signor Viotto and two of his sons were forging ice axes, a process both Tony and Jan found fascinating. Claretta, Bruno informed Tony, was not at home.

"She's gone to the high pastures with the cattle," Tony told Jan when they emerged half an hour later from the foundry, the noise of the hammers ringing in their ears and the glow of the forge dancing in front of their eyeballs. "There'll be no 'hurry-up' bread today, I'm afraid."

"What a shame," said Jan, genuinely disappointed, both about the bread and about the missed chance of having a look inside Bruno Viotto's intriguing house. "But what do you mean, she's with the cattle?"

"In May many of the village women and children take their herds up into the Alps and spend the summer there tending them while they feed on the rich Alpine grass."

"The women and children are up there all alone?" said Jan, staring at the rugged mountain peaks. "What a hard life!"

Tony laughed. "It isn't nearly so primitive as you might imagine." In a sudden burst of enthusiasm, he slipped his arm about her waist. "I have an idea. While I look around for the smith Bruno recommended, why don't you treat yourself to a tour of the village? There's a quite respectable museum at the foot of this street and a number of interesting shops around the corner where you can occupy your time until I'm free."

Jan, thrilled by his touch, nodded eagerly. "I'd like that."

"Good. Then we'll meet for lunch in about an hour. Afterward, if there's time, we'll take a quick run up the mountain and I'll show you the 'hard' life Claretta and the others are leading."

Looking forward to the afternoon, Jan set off, and by lunchtime she had explored the shops, bought several miniature cowbells as souvenirs, and toured the museum, which housed a complete and fascinating display of Premana iron products dating back to the last century, when metal destined to be turned into hardware for the gondola makers of Venice was brought up the mountainside by mules and oxen.

In the quaint little café she and Tony had settled upon as their meeting place, she waited with a cup of very strong coffee and watched through the window while jeeploads of laughing young men started off up the steep road that Tony had indicated they, too, would travel.

"Where is everyone going?" she said when the sturdy waitress came back to refill her cup.

"Ah!" She followed Jan's gaze with a mellow look of her own. "You mean the bridegrooms. They're off to the high pastures to spend Saturday night with their wives." She wagged her head knowingly and showed a toothy grin. "They've only been married since May, and Saturday nights are slow in coming."

Jan's look was blank. "Everyone here gets married in May?"

The waitress shrugged. "Or in September."

"How strange!" Jan exclaimed.

"Not strange at all when you know the reason why." The waitress sat down companionably and leaned her fat elbows on the table. "We all keep cows, you see, and as soon as it's warm in May, all the women who are able go up to the high country with them and they don't come down again until September."

"Yes, I know— Oh!" Jan added, finally seeing her point.

The woman grinned and nodded her head sagely. "If a girl can't make up her mind to get married *before* she goes up, then you can be sure as an Alpine breeze that she's more than ready to tie the knot when she comes down again!"

They laughed together, and Jan thought enviously of the secure feeling a girl must have growing up in a village like Premana with her future so comfortably arranged.

She was still smiling wistfully when Tony arrived.

"Have you had a good time?" he said, taking a place beside her.

"A wonderful time," she answered, though, if she had dared admit it, his joining her was the most wonderful moment of all. Without a trace of the self-consciousness that often plagued her, she launched into a description of what she had seen and done. "And what about you?" she finished. "Did you find the man you were looking for?"

Tony shook his head. "He's up in the mountains somewhere. Perhaps Claretta will know. But before we go up to find him, let's have something to eat, shall we?"

If Jan had thought the road up to Premana perilous, she had no word in her vocabulary of terror for the trail leading from there to the high pastures. Clinging to the door of the jeep, she watched wide-eyed as the sturdy little vehicle with Tony behind the wheel took the rocky switchbacks wide enough for only one lane and carved into the mountainside like a set of gigantic steps. At the end of each lateral stretch he was obliged to throw the jeep into reverse and back up the next section. Turns were out of the question.

"This must be great fun on Sunday afternoons when the bridegrooms are all coming down," said Jan, scared almost speechless each time the wheels sent a cascade of rocks bouncing down onto the road below.

"Ah!" said Tony. "You've heard about the wedding customs of these parts. Quite a practical idea, don't you agree?"

"Unless one happens to want to be married in February or July," she answered, barely able to control her quavering voice. "This is scary, you know—really scary!"

"Move over here by me," he commanded, putting out his arm. "You're making things worse for youself by peering over the edge."

With mixed feelings Jan slid across the seat. All

day she had longed for his touch, but now she discovered she had not entirely forgotten her anguish of the night before, and she wondered as his arm draped carelessly about her shoulder if he was thinking of Maria.

But soon the scent of his sun-warmed skin filled her nostrils and stirred up her senses, and she was sorry when they came to the next reversal and he withdrew his arm to shift into another gear. She stayed next to him, however, and when they were climbing again, he laid his hand briefly on her jean-clad thigh and gave her a smile of such warmth and sweetness that she felt all her mistrust of him melting away. *Perhaps Maria was not so important to him, after all,* she thought, astonished at the intensity of her desire to become a meaningful part of Antonio Torelli's life. The idea was preposterous. It was insane, she knew, and she blamed her yearning on the thin mountain air and the masculine enticement of his nearness. Yet, in spite of the stern lecture she delivered to herself, the longing persisted and grew.

As if Tony sensed what she was feeling, he inquired after a moment, "Still feeling shaky?"

"Not so much," she murmured and pulled her eyes away. "It's beautiful up here, isn't it? So peaceful and quiet. Like the top of the world."

Tony followed her gaze across a valley. "One day I mean to have a cottage on one of these peaks," he said softly.

Jan's heart took a leap. It might be the top of the world, but in some respects it seemed the end of the world, too, and she blurted out, "How will Maria like that?"

His head came around, and he said without a trace of his former warmth, "What has Maria to do with it?"

"I don't know—" *Oh, what an idiot she was!* "I just said that—don't ask me why."

"I *am* asking."

"You and Maria are friends," she stammered. "I suppose I thought—oh, I don't know what I thought—"

"Then perhaps you should stay off the subject," he said curtly. Jan was certain he meant to pursue the matter, but suddenly the road widened. She saw that two other jeeps were parked in a cleared space, and Tony pulled over beside them.

"We walk from here," he said in a clipped monotone, and without glancing back to see if she was following, he struck off up the rocky pathway at a rapid clip.

Thoroughly disgusted with herself for having shattered the mood she had found so exciting, Jan trailed dejectedly behind him.

On both sides there were soft green meadows covered with countless varieties of pastel flowers peeping out of the grass and herds of brown-and-white cattle grazing peacefully.

She was thankful that at least she had heeded Tony's warning and worn jeans and heavy walking shoes. Also, as a concession to him, she had let her hair fall loosely down her back and tied it with a deep blue ribbon. The blue matched his eyes, she thought, trudging along behind him. But if he had noticed it or even that her hair was free from its usual restricting knot, he had given no sign.

Now that she had reminded him of Maria, she thought with a sigh, that, and any future hope that he might have looked at her in the same way he had last night at the dinner table, seemed doomed never to come to pass.

Chapter Ten

The Alpine cottage where Claretta Viotto and the assorted female members of her large family were spending the summer was a sturdy rock dwelling tucked so securely into the mountainside that it seemed to have evolved there like the other slate-colored stones that jutted beside it. A narrow geranium-dotted terrace stretched before the front door, and there girls of varying ages sat knitting at the feet of their comfortably plump elders who were similarly occupied.

When Jan and Tony appeared on the path before them, they rose almost in a body with wide smiles of welcome and hearty greetings.

"Tony!" cried the fair-haired Signora Viotto, who moved forward in a billowing peasant skirt and blue blouse. "What are you doing up here? And who have you brought with you?"

When Tony had introduced Jan and, in explaining their mission, had made clear that the two of them had come alone, there were sighs of disappointment from Claretta and the other women who had hoped for a festive weekend party with their menfolk.

But their hostess quickly recovered her good spirits and told Tony that the man he was looking for had passed by earlier that morning on the way to his own cottage halfway around the mountain. She was sure, she said, that Tony could locate him and be back in time for supper if he started out at once. "The signorina can wait with us," she said, with a smile toward Jan.

Jan would have preferred going with Tony, but he gave her only a glance, said to Claretta, "Teach her to bake *focaccia*," and started up the mountainside alone.

In the kitchen of the cozy cottage whose walls were lined with gleaming copper pots, Jan soon learned that *focaccia* was the "hurry-up" bread that Tony had spoken of earlier, and she was soon absorbed in watching the skillful hands of Claretta Viotto as she worked the unleavened dough—not a "hurry-up" process at all, she discovered, for the industrious housewife spent nearly an hour simply kneading the dough. But at suppertime, when it came off the grill that Claretta had placed over burning grapevine trimmings, it was as delicious as Tony had suggested it would be.

Jan, however, was too disconcerted to fully enjoy it or the rest of the delicious meal the women had prepared. Though she was surrounded at the long wooden table by the happy, friendly faces of the

Viotto womenfolk, she felt lonely and alarmed. She had spent a long afternoon struggling with personal doubts and confusions about Tony, even while she superficially responded to the comfortable hospitality of her hostesses. Darkness had fallen and still he had not returned. Her vivid imagination pictured him at the bottom of some rockpile or stranded dangling over a precipice.

But as she was beginning to despair, he suddenly appeared in the doorway, his cheeks bursting with color from his vigorous hike and seemingly restored to complete good humor.

He had found the man he sought, he told Jan, taking his place beside her at the table and helping himself from the bowls and dishes the women pushed forward. The arrangements were made for the work to be done at the mill as he had hoped. "But"—he turned an appraising glance on Jan—"we can't return to Bellagio tonight. Or even to Premana."

"Oh, no, no!" the women agreed in chorus. The journey down the mountainside was far too perilous. They must not think of attempting it until morning. There was worlds of room in the cottage, Claretta assured them. The smaller girls would enjoy sleeping on pallets in front of the fireplace. Tony could have the room they normally occupied, and Jan, Claretta told her, could share a bed with one of the young married women.

"But not before I show her my moon," Tony said decisively, pushing back from the table. "It was rising spectacularly when I came in." His sensuous gaze slid over Jan, still seated beside him. "Until you've seen the Alps bathed in that particular splendor, you can never say you have seen Italy."

Jan's pulses quickened in appreciation of his softened mood, but she was uncomfortably aware as she rose that every eye at the table was upon them.

"I'll save you a place in my bed, Jan," a dark-haired girl across the table taunted mischievously, "but I won't promise to wait up for you."

Tony shot her a conspiratorial grin. "That's wise of you, *bellisima*."

Amid gales of knowing laughter from the adults around the table, Jan, crimson-faced, was led from the room with Tony's arm wrapped tightly about her waist.

The Alpine meadows, washed in the silvery light of the rising moon—which seemed to Jan twice as big as she had ever seen it—were, as Tony had promised, a sight to behold.

For a time the two of them stood on the terrace in front of the cottage, caught up in the spectacle before them. Then Tony brushed her cheek with his lips. "There's a stream nearby. Let's walk down to it."

Jan fell into step beside him, her blood racing. The tranquility she had felt on the terrace had vanished the moment his lips touched her skin, and in its place the doubts and confusions of the afternoon had returned in full force.

When Tony was near her like this, every dream she had of him seemed possible, but these moments were so fleeting—and the aftermath each time was more painful. All afternoon, watching Claretta

114

knead her bread and listening to the muted chatter of the other women, her mind had gone over every aspect of their relationship.

She was in love with Tony—deeply and hopelessly.

The suddenness with which the realization had come upon her had almost struck her dumb, but as the hours of his absence lengthened, she accepted the truth her heart told her. And yet what hope had she, she thought in anguish, to presume that anything could ever come of her love? There was no place in Tony's life for her, even if he shared her feelings—and the likelihood of that, she was courageous enough to admit, was all but nonexistent.

Still . . . She stole a glance across at him, strolling confidently along beside her. Why, if he cared nothing for her, did he continue to draw her into situations like this one? At dinner the evening before he had admitted that he found her attractive. *Stunning* was his word. He had convinced her that a part of him did care for her, but the tedious patterns of male-female behavior that eventually might—or might *not*—lead him to tell her so, or perhaps even to realize it himself, were foreign to her. The heroines in the books she read were able to draw men out as easily as they breathed, but female wiles had never worked for her.

What was she to do? she wondered helplessly. Must she go on loving Tony from afar, able only to hope against hope that he might one day turn from Maria and bring his love to her?

Tony broke into her thoughts. "Why so quiet?" he chided gently, and with a start she realized they had reached their destination. Before them the stream

Tony had spoken of danced its crystalline way over mossy rocks, and in the scrubby growth beside it Jan could hear the sleepy twitterings of birds.

"I was thinking," she answered him.

"Of what?"

She moistened her lips. *Did she dare tell him?*

Before she could decide, his arms came around her. Pulling her down into the soft grass, he sought out her lips hungrily. As always, his were devilishly persuasive lips that at once scattered reason to the winds. Their hot, moist movement set her senses reeling, and the uncertainties of the afternoon fled before the erotic pressure of his mouth. Its warmth and urgency intoxicated her. Instinctively she arched against him and, with unconscious subtle movements of her own, she celebrated the scent of his skin, his hypnotic touch, his body hardening against hers.

Feverishly his hands slid across her hips, his embrace tightened. She heard him moan, and passion blazed quickly between them. Afire with ardor, Jan let the world slip away. Tony was hers! His mouth, she fantasized as he brought down his lips again, was a cup from which life itself was transmitted to her.

Minute piled on minute. Their need for each other intensified and they clung together, weightless, mindless, Tony's heartbeat stirring the soft swell of her breasts as under his sinuous, skillful touch he explored the labyrinths of her desire. Within Jan, ecstasy unfurled—an exotic, convoluted flower, blooming in this one magic moment only for them.

Dimly Jan became aware of how perilous their

mood was, of the dangerous path they were travel-
ing. She was not prepared to tread it, she knew, but,
seemingly powerless to halt their transit, she felt
herself slipping deeper into erotic abandonment as
Tony's breathing thickened.

Then, suddenly, she sensed a break in the rhythm
of their sharing—a movement—and with a jolt she
realized that Tony had brought her arms down from
his neck. Effortlessly he drew apart from her and lay
back in the grass, studying the stars, his hands
beneath his head.

In the strained silence that fell between them, Jan
heard his breathing return to normal. Finally he
said, as casually as if they had not kissed at all, "Did
you enjoy this afternoon?"

Jan ran her tongue across her throbbing lips.
"Yes." She swallowed. "The women were kind to
me." Then, with a courage she was far from feeling,
she forced her eyes around to his. "But I think they
are wondering who I am."

Idly he plucked a stem of grass. "I told them who
you are."

"That's not what I mean. They're wondering if—"

He broke in crisply. "You are a designer for
Torelli Silks. What else do they need to know?"

He was saying, she realized through her pain, *that
their relationship as employer and employee was all
there was to know.* Her heart warned that she should
accept that. But he had held her too closely
. . . touched her too passionately . . .

She turned and looked squarely at him. "Why did
you kiss me?"

His depthless eyes traveled over her. Then with a slow smile he said, "Because I wanted to." He paused. "Why did you let me?"

"Because I enjoyed it."

"Well, then—" He laughed softly and leaned toward her. "We both have our answers." His arm came around her shoulder, and he started to pull her back down into the grass, but she stiffened in resistance.

"Please don't."

"Why not?" His tone said more clearly than words that she had been eager enough a moment before.

But she held on to her determination to set things straight between them once and for all. "Each time we are together," she said evenly, "I become more convinced of our need to speak frankly to each other."

"Really?" His surprise was apparent, but only for a moment. "Why?"

"For the very reason that you have to *ask* why," she answered in a muffled voice, but she kept her chin high.

"I don't know what you're talking about," he said carelessly.

"I don't think you want to know."

He sat up. "Stop talking in riddles," he demanded edgily.

"I'll put it more plainly, then. I think it's unfair and improper of you to go on taking me into your arms and kissing me when you have plans to marry another woman."

He drew his breath in sharply. "What?"

"I said—"

But he cut her off. "I heard what you said." He gave a low, incredulous laugh. "I just don't believe it."

For a wild, incredible moment Jan wondered if that could mean that he did *not* intend to marry Maria, but in another moment Tony's scornful tone snuffed out her hope.

"I can't believe that one or two kisses have brought us to this kind of discussion."

Despair knifed through Jan, but she held steady. "It's unfortunate that I have to remind you there have been more than one or two kisses."

"What's unfortunate is that there were any at all!" he muttered. "There wouldn't have been, I can assure you, if I had had any idea you were so naïve as to think they were leading up to a proposal of marriage."

"I haven't said that!"

"Then, by heaven, what *are* you saying?"

Her throat tightened as she fought her tears. "Only that if you don't care for me you should stop behaving as if you do."

"Good Lord!" he exploded angrily. "I've kissed you twice—three times at the most—and you jump to the conclusion that I'm in love with you. Where have you been, girl? This is the twentieth century!"

"Human sensitivities are the same in all centuries," she answered, barely able to keep the tremor from her voice. "As to where I've been—you know that well enough. I've been nowhere. But that's not to say I don't know that discussions of this sort between men and women are ordinarily more subtle than this one."

He looked at her in openmouthed astonishment.

"But *you* ought to know," she went on, her chin trembling, "that subtlety is not my style. I have to be sure of exactly where I stand."

For a long moment he stared at her as if he hoped she might simply disappear. Then he said in a low, carefully controlled voice, "You talk of sensitivity—then how can you be so insensitive yourself as not to realize how absurd this is?" He softened a little. "Look here—I don't want to hurt you, but it's ridiculous for you to have assumed that I would feel anything more for you than"—he lifted his wide shoulders—"than for any other girl I've kissed."

Her voice broke. "There've been quite a few, I'm sure!"

"Yes—there have been!" His calm gave way to angry exasperation. "And I sincerely hope there'll be many more."

White-faced, Jan said, "Do you intend to marry Maria?"

"I don't think that's any of your business!"

Scrambling to her feet, she said in a choked voice, "I'm going in."

Tony rose swiftly beside her and grabbed her wrists. "You're not going into Claretta's cottage in that mood! You and I are going back to Bellagio."

"Tonight?" she said in disbelief. "Down that awful road?"

Without answering, he started off down the path, pulling her along with him.

"You brought me to this place because you meant to make love to me, didn't you?" she accused as she stumbled after him. "That's why everyone in the cottage laughed. They knew what you were up to, and now you don't want to face them." Her voice struck out like a whiplash. "Is this your usual summer pastime? Seducing girls on mountaintops?"

He halted, jerking her hard against his chest. "If I had wanted to make love to you, I would have, no matter where we were. One place is as good as another when the woman is as willing as you are."

Jan gasped and tore herself free, but he had withered her with his blast. He was justified in saying that—she had forgotten everything when he was holding her in his arms. What she might have done if he had not broken away, she was afraid to ask herself.

Tony spoke contemptuously. "Are you coming? Or do I have to drag you?"

"I'd rather sleep on a stone than go down that mountain in the dark!"

"Look around you," he sneered. "It's bright as day."

It was true, she saw with shocked numbness. While they had argued, the moon had risen to its full height and sent every shadow scurrying. *Tony had bested her on every count and stripped her of her pride as well.* Trailing along after him, she realized with bitter clarity that the feminine wiles she had long held in contempt had their place, after all—they were a woman's only defense against the male. She had been stupid enough to close her eyes to that. She deserved now to have her heart broken.

Chapter Eleven

Wearier than she had ever been in her life, Jan slept until nearly noon on Sunday morning. When she awoke, eyes still swollen from weeping, her first thought was of what a fool she had made of herself the night before.

What must Tony think of her?

Coming down out of the mountains, he had been too preoccupied with mastering the road to pursue their argument. Then, once they were past Premana and winding through the valley, she had turned away from him, pretending sleep, and no conversation had been possible then either.

But this evening—or in the morning—she must deliver to him the designs she had promised. How should she act when she saw him again?

Then she remembered dully that it really didn't

matter. Tony had dismissed her. If she were to salvage even a shred of pride, she would need to behave as if nothing had happened.

Actually nothing had, she thought with a renewed ache. The kisses Tony had given her meant no more to him than if he had kissed the back of her sketchbook. She had startled him with her remarks afterward—and angered him, too, but only momentarily. In the end, all she had done was to reinforce her image as the prim and proper Miss Martin he despised so. Her moments of reckless abandon he quite obviously had dismissed as a ploy on Jan's part to start him thinking of marriage, and he had certainly made clear how absurd he thought *that* was!

By now, no doubt, if he remembered at all what had happened, he thought of it as another amusing display of naïveté on Jan's part. Either he was laughing at her or he had forgotten she existed. The thing *she* must never forget again was that in Tony's eyes her only importance was her work.

Her work!

Groaning, she pulled herself out of bed. The designs she had promised Tony were finished, but she would do well, she knew, to check them over and polish them up before she submitted them. Particularly now that she knew they might soon go into production. Better to get at them now and get her mind off depressing thoughts of Tony. Besides, as unpredictable as he was, he might knock on her door in half an hour and demand them, even though he had said he was not returning to Como until Monday.

Feeling more exhausted by the minute, Jan pulled on jeans and a smock. *Tea first,* she told herself and headed toward the stairs. But when she reached them, a strange sense of uneasiness turned her steps upward.

Just a quick look in the studio. Then, if there were changes to be made in some of the drawings, she could be thinking about them while she had her breakfast . . .

Still half asleep, she stumbled toward her work-table, but when she reached it the design book she sought was not on top nor beneath the layers of ivory paper that held other drawings. Casually she searched the drawers. *If one of them did not disclose the book, another would,* she thought, but her throat tightened as drawer after drawer revealed nothing.

Wide awake now, she sank into a chair, fighting off a surge of panic. *What had she done with the designs? When had she had them last?*

Painstakingly she forced herself to retrace the events of the day before yesterday. *She had been ill-humored* . . . she remembered that clearly enough . . . *and worried about the clothes she had brought from Jean LeCou's. Reading. She had tried that . . . she had come up here—* But of course! The swimming pool!

Hastily she made for the stairs. She had a habit of taking her sketchbooks everywhere. Though she could not recall having done so, perhaps she had taken the design book down to the pool. She licked her lips, thinking of that possibility. The heavy Mediterranean dew had fallen twice since then.

Worse, the book might have gone into the water with her when Tony had so ungraciously shoved her in.

Barefoot, she sped across the stones of the courtyard, heedless of the noonday sun that scorched their surface. *If the book was ruined . . . if she couldn't find it at all . . . how would she ever meet Tony's deadline?*

All at once she halted as from behind the hedge of pittosporum that surrounded the pool, a trill of feminine laughter floated. *Was that Maria?* Jan's hand flew to her hair. *She hadn't even combed it!*

Ducking quickly behind the hedge, Jan peered through the glossy leaves. Just as she had feared, Maria was there, stretched out on the tile coping—with Tony beside her. He lay with his back toward Maria, while she—up on one elbow—lazily massaged oil into his tanned shoulders. She wore the same abbreviated swimsuit she had worn when Jan had discovered her on the marble steps, and she looked, Jan thought with a sickening wave of envy, even more bewitching than she had that day.

Maria's voice drifted over the hedge. "What a sleepyhead you are," she chided Tony. "You haven't said two words since we came out. If I'd known what dull company you'd be, I'd have stayed in Venice."

Tony sat up, and Jan saw with quickening pulse that he appeared as washed out and weary as herself. "If you had spent half the night driving through the mountains, you'd be sleepy, too," he answered irritably.

"It serves you right," said Maria loftily. "If you'd

been here waiting when I arrived, you wouldn't be suffering now. Whose idea was it to drive up to that wretched village anyway? Yours? Or was that something the mouse from Kansas thought up?"

The mouse from Kansas! Jan let out a gasp of outrage. Maria appeared not to notice, but Tony's eyes immediately swung toward the hedge. Jan froze as his keen-eyed gaze raked the pungent cover she crouched behind. Then, with relief, she saw him yawn and turn again toward Maria.

"Actually," he told her in a somewhat louder tone than before, "it was quite an interesting trip. Too bad you weren't along."

Maria arched her eyebrows. "Thank heaven I wasn't. I can't think of anything worse than being stuck all day with dear Miss Martin in that mucky little village."

"Miss Martin is quite an authority on everything," Tony replied lazily. "She's a reader, you know. In fact"—his languid gaze went back to the hedge—"she's a veritable encyclopedia of boring detail."

Behind the pittosporum, Jan bit her lip and seethed. *Oh, if ever she had him alone again . . . !*

Tony went on in the same elevated tone. "Statues, churches, ice axes—there's nothing she feels is beyond the range of comment—and she comments endlessly. All one has to do to get her started is choose a subject."

Maria turned up a pair of pouting lips. "I choose you, darling. Please, if you don't mind, I don't care if I never hear of Minnie Mouse again."

Tony laughed, and then, staring straight into the

hedge, he reached out for Maria. Pulling her into his arms, he dropped his face to hers and delivered a long, lingering kiss that sent Jan flying back up the path, blinded to everything except the image of their two sleek bodies molded together by passion.

Inside the tower once again, Jan dropped in a trembling, dejected heap at the foot of the staircase. The picture of Tony and Maria locked in each other's arms had burned itself into her brain. She would see it, she knew, until the day she died.

And good enough for you! she told herself savagely. As long as she could keep the image fresh in her mind, she should be safe from ever believing again that she was in love with Antonio Torelli.

He was a faithless, arrogant egotist who cared nothing for the feelings of others. *Even if Maria wins him,* she thought with a measure of bitter satisfaction, *he will never be hers alone.*

But thoughts of Tony's fickle nature brought only momentary comfort, and Jan sat huddled for a quarter of an hour on the steps, vainly trying to blot from her memory the persuasive power of Tony's kiss and the broken dreams of him that no power on earth could mend now.

Gradually, however, the determined spirit that had helped her through many an unpleasant scene with Aunt Elizabeth reasserted itself. Tony would regret that he had treated her so badly, she vowed. Before she was through he would recognize her as the most brilliant designer Torelli Silks had ever known. He would come crawling on his knees, begging her to stay in Italy. Oh, what a joy it would be to scorn him then—and to move on to a rival company! Through the years other designers had chosen as their logos turtles, jeweled crowns, even misproportioned crocodiles, but hers would be the most renowned logo of all—a proud Kansas mouse! In a few years, Jan fantasized, all of Europe would beg to have that imprint, and each time Antonio Torelli saw it he would curse Maria Bertani and his own stupidity.

But before any of that could happen— Jan got up with a sigh. Before she brought Tony to his knees, she had to find her design book. Suddenly a picture of Maria standing in the middle of the studio in her swimsuit flipping through pages flashed across Jan's mind. *It was Maria who had had the sketchbook last!*

Just as swiftly, however, that image was replaced with another—of Maria passing the book back to Jan with a disdainful smile. *It was her own hands,* she recalled, *that had held it last.* In a frenzy of frustration Jan looked down at her fingers curled tightly into fists. If only they could speak and clear up this alarming mystery!

Then, almost as if Providence had heard her plea, the tower door swung open and Allegra, the maid, stepped in out of the sunshine. Seeing Jan huddled on the stairs, she drew back in surprise, but before she could speak, Jan rose and eagerly fired a question at her.

"Allegra—when you came to clean the other day—the day you brought the yellow towels and the fresh potted plants—did you go up to the studio?"

Allegra blinked. "No, signorina. It was Wednesday that I cleaned the studio."

"I know," said Jan desperately. "But I thought perhaps— Did you straighten the bedroom then?" If by some chance she had brought the book down herself— She could have laid it on the bed or the dresser, and Allegra could have put it away somewhere—

But Allegra shook her head again. "I straightened the room while you were walking that morning," the girl said patiently. "All was done when I came with the towels. Was much later, signorina." She flashed two rows of brilliant white teeth. "I zip in. I zip out."

Jan smiled faintly in acknowledgment of Allegra's American slang, but her anxiety increased. "I lost something that day. A sketchbook. You're certain you didn't move it somewhere?"

Allegra was horrified. "Oh, *no*, signorina! When I clean, I leave everything exactly as they are. Signor Torelli demands that."

That was true, Jan knew. Nothing except dust was ever disturbed by Allegra's tidy ministrations.

With a sigh Jan rose and gave the girl a wan smile. "I've overlooked it, then. I'll simply have to search again."

They went up the stairs together, Allegra turning into the bedroom on the second floor to change the linens, and Jan continuing upward to search the studio again.

But in a few minutes, Allegra poked her head above the top step. "I have thought of something," she said with a bright smile.

"You've found my book!" exclaimed Jan.

"No—but I know who you must ask. Ann Janell. She was here. She may know."

Ann Janell, Maria's maid. Jan recalled the sullen girl leaning near the tower door with her shopping bag, and her hopes sank. "Thanks very much, but I'm afraid Ann Janell can't help."

"But she was here!" Allegra insisted.

"I know. She was waiting for me. I brought a parcel from Bellagio for her mistress."

Allegra giggled suddenly. "Ann Janell was very angry at her mistress afterward. All the way to Bellagio she is forced to walk because there is no petrol in Signorina Bertani's automobile."

Jan sucked in her breath. *The gasoline!* She had not thought of it once since Maria's warning that there might not be enough to get back to the villa. "This was on Thursday?" she said, vainly hoping it was not.

But Allegra, still glowing with pleasure at the haughty Ann Janell's misfortune, confirmed that it was. "There is one station on the road to Bellagio." Her laughter bubbled over. "But it does not pump petrol on Thursday."

Poor Ann Janell, thought Jan, listening as Allegra's laughter faded down the stairwell. *My fault. Everything is my fault . . . the lost design book . . . the lost love of Tony . . .*

But that was wrong too, she chided herself. Tony's love had never been hers to lose. The episode at the swimming pool had pointed that up plainly enough.

Tears filled her eyes. *Oh, where was that all-important sketchbook?* In only a few hours Tony would appear, demanding to see the work she had bragged about. What would "the greatest designer in Europe" say then when she had nothing to show him?

Chapter Twelve

The lights in the tower studio burned all night. They were still burning at six o'clock on Monday morning when Jan came numbly down the stairs, a manila portfolio under her arm and inside it a dozen new sketches. She had worked straight through until dawn—a week's labor compressed into sixteen exhausting hours.

In the kitchen she laid the portfolio on the table and wearily filled the teakettle. When had she eaten last? she wondered dimly. Yesterday? The day before?

For all she knew it might have been at Claretta Viotto's table in the Alpine meadows. Too many miserable hours had passed since her world had fallen apart after that meal to know what had happened since. But one thing she did know: she didn't care if she never ate again.

But at least the work was done. Gratefully she glanced at the bulging portfolio. Thank heaven for that, at least.

While the kettle steamed, she drew out the design pages once more and studied them wearily, but with eyes still sharp enough to see that they were excellent. They were, in fact, superior to anything she had ever done before.

Perhaps exhaustion had inspired her, she thought grimly. But more likely desperation had. Though she had searched the tower from top to bottom, the sketchbook was nowhere to be found. She had wanted to die then, but the only thing she had left—her pride in her work—had been on the line. Through sheer fortitude, she had managed not to betray it.

Drawing from her memories of the drive to Premana and on up to the high meadows, she had created a sparkling, surrealistic array of nature patterns: dainty Alpine flowers juxtaposed against the harsh perpendicular inclines; intriguing etchings of barks and mosses in startling colors; abstracted clouds and mountain peaks in delicate apricot and peach.

Perhaps what had happened had been a blessing in disguise, she comforted herself. Eventually the old sketchbook was bound to turn up, and then, like cash in the bank, she could draw from it, incorporating those earlier designs in future work. But for today—for Tony to take back to Como for her first test run—she had pulled from herself a power she had not known she possessed.

She was still studying her work a quarter of an

hour later when she heard a knock. *Tony?* Her hands flew to her unwashed face. Her intention had been to take her tea upstairs and avoid seeing him when he came by, calling down that he would find the finished work on the table. Since yesterday she hadn't changed her clothes or even combed her hair.

But what did any of that really matter? Tony had trifled with her deepest emotions; he had deliberately mocked her when she was hiding in the hedge by the pool. What was there left for him to see or to know about her that he had not already rejected?

When the knock came once again, more impatiently, she dragged herself to the door and threw it open.

Tony entered without ceremony, his brows jumping together when his eyes lit on Jan's wan face and tight mouth.

"What have you done to yourself?" he demanded.

Brushing a lock of hair from her eyes, Jan noticed that Tony, though freshly shaved and showered and impeccably attired in a dark gray business suit, appeared as drawn as she, and she turned away toward the squealing teakettle with a surge of satisfaction. Whatever had kept him awake—Maria or a bad conscience or possibly both—served him right.

"One of the things I *haven't* done," she replied flatly, "is to fix myself a cup of tea. Will you join me?"

He ignored the invitation. "You need more than tea," he said with annoyance. "You've been up all night, haven't you?"

"What if I have?"

"You told me the designs were finished," he accused. "Obviously they weren't."

"They're finished now," she answered with a stubborn thrust of her chin. "So it doesn't really matter when I did them, does it?"

"I don't appreciate being lied to."

Jan whirled around from the stove. "Look at them!" she challenged. "If you still feel cheated, I'll be happy to go back to Paris at once."

With an angry flush, he scooped up the portfolio and pulled out a heavy sheet. Then another—and another. He was silent so long studying the pages that Jan's heart began to pound. Had she been wrong? Were they actually terrible, and she had been too tired to realize it?

But when at last Tony raised his eyes, they were glowing with approval. "I've never seen anything better!" he exclaimed, barely able to contain his excitement. "There's no question now that we can regain our status in the silk trade—and more. You've done superb work."

Tears of relief burned at Jan's eyelids, but she took refuge from her emotions in a sharp retort. "Maria may not think so."

"Maria won't see them," he answered crisply, shoving the pages back into the portfolio. "She's still asleep, I imagine."

Pain shot through Jan. *In your bed?* she wondered.

"That's where *you* should be," said Tony, as if he read her thoughts. He peered intently at her. "Lord, you look terrible. You aren't ill, are you?"

The concern in his tone was more than Jan could bear, and she fled toward the stairs.

He called after her. "I'll have breakfast sent over—"

"Leave me alone!" she cried shrilly from the shadows of the stairs. "Please—just go away and leave me alone!"

The days after Tony's departure for Como were a nightmare to Jan. Despite every psychological trick she could devise, Tony stayed on her mind. She had believed that the scene beside the swimming pool when he had kissed Maria would erase forever her love for him, but to her distress she found it only increased her longing. Hers was a hopeless, futile love, she knew, but it burned ever brighter inside her heart, threatening to consume her.

Her only refuge was in establishing a strict routine, and she adhered to that faithfully, going through the motions each day of living a normal life.

She rose early, as had always been her custom, and capitalizing on a promise extracted from Tony before they had quarreled, she took the Borzoi, Nappy, on a long walk through the woods. The dog was good company, sensitive and warmly affectionate, and she took comfort in the quiet hour she spent with him.

Afterward she had tea and toast in the tower kitchen and then she worked, stopping at ten for a swim in the pool and again at one for a lunch consisting of whatever delicacies the cook sent over from the main house. Gradually her appetite had returned, but generally she ate with a book beside her plate, finding it easier to read about the plights of others than to trust her thoughts to her own troubles.

In the afternoons she worked steadily, dreading as the sun sank lower the approach of night. The stars over Lake Como, she had discovered, were bigger and more brilliant than she had ever observed them to be in Kansas, and the gentle twitterings of the nightbirds awakened within her a deep sense of melancholy. She did her best to stay away from the tower windows, but invariably before the evenings were over she found herself drawn to the glittering display of lights from Bellagio, and she caught herself dreaming of Tony, feeling herself enclosed in his embrace, lifting her face for his kiss, swaying in his arms as soft dance music played . . .

Finally, toward the end of the week, as she was indulging in one such fantasy, it came to her with a shock that she had been so absorbed in her misery that she had forgotten entirely about the enormous bill she had run up at Jean LeCou's.

Breaking her routine the next morning, she dressed carefully in her old linen skirt and white blouse, and hailing the gardener as he set off for town, she begged a ride.

Jolting along in his dingy truck, she reminded herself that she had never worn the madras suit nor the red organza ball gown. It was foolish to keep them hanging in the closet, particularly now that there was no chance that she would ever wear them, but regardless of that she found herself unable to part with them. *Perhaps when she was back in Paris,* she thought guiltily, but in her heart she knew that she was holding on to the clothes in the same way she was holding on to her old dreams of Tony. *One day he might take her dancing. One day she might dine with him in the madras suit and see his eyes light up with desire again. . . .*

By the time she had arrived at the shop, her spirits were soaring with imaginary plans, but the moment she stepped inside they vanished like a puff of smoke when she saw who was there ahead of her—Maria, lounging idly near a rack of exquisite chiffon creations a clerk was showing her.

When her eyes fell on Jan, she inquired lazily, "Oh, window-shopping?"

"I've come to look at dresses," Jan retorted sharply.

"Maybe you should look at the price tags first," Maria said with a laugh.

But at that moment the clerk who had waited on Jan before approached her with a wide smile. "Ah, signorina, how delightful to see you again. Our new shipment of gowns has just arrived from France— beautiful things just to your taste. May I show them to you?"

Maria gawked, and Jan, with the sweet taste of revenge on her tongue, answered smoothly, "Why, yes, I'd love to see them."

Jan dawdled as long as she could in the dressing room, trying on one gown after another and peering out in between times to see if Maria had gone.

Each time, however, she discovered her beautiful rival still seated in a lounge chair, plainly determined to wait her out. At last, in desperation, Jan paraded out into the display area wearing a free-flowing crepe de chine dinner dress and hoping fervently that Maria would be annoyed enough at the sight of her to give up her vigil.

But Maria only surveyed her coolly and said in a bored tone, "That doesn't become you. Your make-up and your hair are too old-fashioned for a dress like that."

The clerk, who had lavishly praised Jan's appearance in the dressing room, stared askance at Maria, but Jan, keeping her temper under control, said calmly, "Hair and makeup can always be altered. It's the cut of the dress that must stand as it is." She turned back to the clerk. "This one is beautifully cut," she said decisively. "I'll take it."

The astonished look on Maria's face was almost worth the sickening feeling Jan experienced the moment the words were out. *What was she thinking of? She was already in debt up to her eyebrows!* On trembling legs she made her way back to the dressing room, and in a few minutes—again wearing her old linen skirt and blouse—she found herself seated behind an Oriental screen that set off the bookkeeping department from the rest of the shop.

If only Maria would leave! she thought desperately, watching the expensive gown being folded into a shiny white box. Finally she said in a quavering voice, "About my account—"

The dark-eyed woman behind the desk smiled.

"All taken care of, just as you requested. We appreciate so much, Signorina Martin, your prompt instructions to channel your account through the firm of Torelli Silks. It simplifies our bookkeeping when our patrons are as considerate as you."

Jan stared blankly at her. "Torelli Silks." She swallowed. "Yes . . ."

The woman stood up. "Shall we deliver this?" She picked up the box containing Jan's dress. "Or would you prefer to take it with you?"

Torelli Silks was paying for her clothes? Jan licked her lips. No one could have ordered that but Tony—and he must have done so when he still believed he could profit from such a move! Her first impulse was to run from the shop, but her wildly darting gaze settled on Maria beyond the screen, impatiently tapping her foot.

Blindly Jan reached for the box. "I'll take it." If it took a hundred years to pay for those few yards of silk, Jan vowed, it would be worth it to emerge with the dress under her arm and wipe that self-satisfied smirk off Maria Bertani's lips!

If Maria was surprised to see that Jan had actually purchased the gown that she considered too outrageously priced even for herself, she was quick to recover her poise when Jan appeared.

"I'll give you a ride back to the villa," she said as the two of them emerged from the shop. "I want to see what kind of work you've been doing."

"I really need the walk," Jan protested, but when Maria opened the door of her smart little car and stood imperiously beside it, Jan reluctantly crawled in.

"I'll just whip by my own place first," said Maria when they were on their way, "and leave some instructions about dinner. Then I'll drop you off."

"I don't think you'll be interested in my work," Jan said quickly. "It hasn't gone well this week."

"Oh?" Maria lifted an eyebrow. "Why not?"

Jan made her shrug nonchalant. "That's the way things turn out sometimes."

"I should think that, if you're as talented as Tony seems to believe, ideas would pop straight out of your head onto the page."

Maria's sarcasm started a queasy feeling in Jan's stomach. Maria couldn't care less what kind of work she was doing. What did she really want?

"Well, whatever you're doing," Maria went on, with a wry look at the box in Jan's lap, "it seems to pay well."

Jan relaxed a little. Perhaps that was it. Maria only wanted a chance to dig her about the dress. "It's fun to be able to buy pretty clothes."

"Yes, isn't it?" said Maria. "It's one of my favorite pastimes. You haven't seen my place, have you?" she went on as she whipped the sleek little car into a shaded driveway and pulled it to a stop in front of an enormous stone mansion.

Jan started to get out, thinking that the remark was the prelude to an invitation to have a look at Maria's villa, but Maria stopped her with a sultry smile.

"Just stay where you are. I'll only be a minute."

What a master she was in the art of making other people feel insignificant, fumed Jan as she waited in the car. *I'd like to tell her,* she thought, *that I don't care for her gloomy old barn anyway!*

Unlike the warm, welcoming look of Tony's villa, Maria's stone fortress faced out at the water with a closed, dismal facade that made it hard to imagine that anyone behind its thick walls could ever be happy. Gazing at it, Jan felt a little smug about her own pleasant situation at the Villa Torelli, and she was in a better mood when Maria finally emerged again, bearing a large canvas tote bag which she slung carelessly into the back seat before she slid behind the wheel.

"I've shopping to do," she said airily. "Poor cook. I've a guest coming for dinner, and I forgot to warn her. I'll have to go back to town again."

"What a shame," Jan murmured, not quite able to believe that Maria would condescend to market for the cook, but at the same time puzzled why she would say so if it weren't the truth. "Why not drop me off on the main road, then? I'll walk on up to the villa from there."

Maria gave her a superior smile. "You really don't want me to see your work, do you? It must be pretty terrible."

"Not at all," bristled Jan, smarting under the pointed remark. "I don't want to bore you, that's all."

Maria paced the studio restlessly, but she was not bored. Her sharp, inquisitive glances seemed to be everywhere at once, and Jan grew uneasy watching her as she strutted back and forth, picking up the sheets of half-finished designs Jan had brought out for her and then laying them down again wherever she happened to be.

Finally, tossing the one she had studied the longest onto the table, she laid a slender wrist against her forehead. "Fetch me a glass of Perrier, please," she said to Jan in a tone she might use for a servant. "Looking at these things has exhausted me."

"I'm afraid I haven't any Perrier," Jan replied stiffly, "but I can bring up a glass of plain water from the kitchen if you'd like."

Maria flopped on the couch beside her tote bag. "Yes, do that. Anything—but hurry. I feel a little faint."

Concerned, but not entirely convinced that Maria was ill, Jan sped off down the stairs. Wryly she wondered if it really was her designs that had brought on this sudden spell. Clearly Maria had no real interest in them, yet she insisted on inspecting them. Was she trying to impress Tony with her knowledge? Or did she simply enjoy ordering people about?

Still puzzling the question, Jan filled a glass at the kitchen sink and had started back up the stairs when a thought so astonishing came into her brain that she felt as if an explosion had occurred there.

Maria was the thief!

Dumbfounded, she stood motionless on the stairs. Of course. Everything fit perfectly. Maria attended

143

all the design meetings . . . she had Tony's absolute trust . . . *It was Maria who was robbing Torelli Silks of its designs and its reputation!*

She's up there now, thought Jan in panic, *stuffing her bag full with my work!*

Water sloshed over her wrist as she raced up the curving stairway, but when she emerged breathlessly at the top, Maria was exactly where she had left her, stretched out on the couch with her eyes closed.

"Ah, you're back," she said when she heard Jan's step. With a wan smile, she sat up and took the glass from Jan's outstretched hand. "I'm feeling better. It's the heat, I suppose. So unusual for this time of year." She took a sip of the water and raised herself off the couch. "My headache has eased, but I think I'll go back to the villa and lie down for a bit anyway."

"Yes!" said Jan, her eyes darting around the room. "Let the cook do her own shopping!" Scarcely aware that she was even speaking, she counted off in her brain the number of design sheets visible in various parts of the room. *Three were missing! Which three? Where were they? Should she demand to inspect the tote bag? What if she were wrong?* Dimly she heard Maria's voice.

"Don't bother to come down with me. I'll let myself out."

"You're sure you don't mind?" Jan responded mechanically.

"Quite sure. You get on with your work." Maria's lips turned up in a strange little smile. "I'll just take it very slowly."

Jan could scarcely wait for Maria's head to disappear into the stairwell to make a dash for the desk. Her fingers flew through the stacks of ivory paper there. *Twelve, thirteen—one more. Where was it?* She went back across the room to the table. *Not here. The wastebasket? She wouldn't put it past her!* But the wastebasket was empty.

Down below a car started beside the moat. Jan tensed. *If she has my sketch—* Then her eyes fell on the mantel. The missing drawing lay there, half hidden behind an arrangement of rich red geraniums Allegra had placed there the morning before.

Weak with relief, Jan sank down on the couch. *So much for snap judgments,* she thought, feeling as if she might faint herself. *It had all seemed so logical on the stairs—*

Except for the motive! she thought suddenly. A hoarse laugh came up from her throat. How stupid to have suspected Maria. Maria was a major stockholder in Torelli Silks. She would be killing the goose that laid her golden eggs if she deliberately damaged the firm's reputation. *And yet . . .*

Jan stared into the fireplace banked with greenery. Maria had behaved so strangely. Why had she bothered to come here at all today? And that fainting act was definitely phony. The sketchbook was still missing, too, and that was peculiar. . . .

The uneasy, unnamable feeling that had disturbed Jan earlier crept over her again. She felt that Maria was definitely not to be trusted, but perhaps that was only because she disliked her so intensely.

Restlessly, Jan moved to the window. Through a

clearing at the end of the drive, she saw Maria's sleek little car turning onto the main road. *Maria was Tony's choice,* she thought dully. *I'm jealous, that's all.* But still the annoying feeling persisted, and even after she had seated herself at the table and taken up her work again, she continued to see Maria's farewell smirk.

Chapter Thirteen

Several weeks passed and Jan heard nothing more from Maria. She heard nothing from Tony, either, and as the days went by the fear grew within her that her work had been rejected in Como. Perhaps even now she had been fired. Perhaps Tony had simply neglected to notify her.

Nevertheless, she clung stubbornly to the belief that her work was good, and day by day she applied herself diligently to the creation of new designs, determined that if she were still in the employ of Torelli Silks she would be prepared if and when Tony did finally reappear.

Though depression hung heavily over her as the days dragged by, one unexpected event did have the effect, at least briefly, of lifting her spirits.

The missing design book turned up at last.

On the morning after Maria's peculiar fainting spell, Allegra, cleaning in Jan's bedroom, discovered the book jammed down behind the fireplace screen. Her dismay was equaled only by Jan's delight.

"Each day I have dusted in this place!" the girl insisted. "And now where there was not a book, there *is* a book. This cannot be!"

"It's quite all right, Allegra," said Jan. She felt that the little maid's embarrassment at having her carelessness found out had caused her to lie, and Jan knew that she was lax in not dealing sternly with Allegra, but she was too relieved at recovering the book to mar her joy with an unpleasant scene. "I should have noticed it there myself," she said soothingly. "In the future we shall both be more careful."

Somewhat mollified, Allegra went back to her work, but she continued to talk to herself about the mysterious reappearance of the book, and finally Jan took it down to the kitchen to study it. While she drank a cup of tea, she leafed through its pages, noticing first with surprise and then with growing delight how well done the work was.

Before the book disappeared, she had believed the drawings were good, but now she saw they were even better than she remembered. One in particular caught her eye, and she found herself going back to it again and again.

It was the wheat, grapevine, and violet intertwining that had caught Tony's eye the day he had first kissed her. All of the other drawings, she saw, could do with a bit of polishing here and there, but this one—this one was perfect as it was. It was a treasure. It deserved to be guarded as such, she decided.

As soon as Allegra had finished her work and gone back to the main house, Jan climbed the stairs and, unlocking the armoire in her bedroom, she placed the sketchbook on a shelf inside. When the door was locked again, she took a thin silver chain of Aunt Elizabeth's from her jewelry drawer and, stringing the key on it, hung it around her neck.

It was not the key to her heart, she thought with an ache as she fingered the worn old metal. That belonged to Tony—though he would never know it. But, nevertheless, the key to the armoire was the key to her future. It was clearer each day that there would be no man in her future if the man was not to be Tony—and that, of course, was not even to be considered. She must take care of her work now. Her work was all she had.

Reminding herself of that depressed her, and though she chided herself for being ungrateful for the recovery of the missing sketchbook, the sun that had shone briefly for her ducked behind a cloud, and for days afterward she had to fight harder than ever to keep her mind off Tony.

Would he ever come back? she kept wondering. *Why was he staying away so long? Was Maria with him in Como? Was he the guest Maria had been expecting for dinner? Had he stayed that weekend at the villa with her?*

To keep herself sane through the torment of her questioning, Jan resolutely walked with Nappy. She swam in the pool. She worked. In the evenings, which otherwise might have been the most painful hours of all, she marched herself over to the main house and read in Tony's library until she was so sleepy she could hardly find her way back to the tower.

Except for the absence of romance on the library shelves, Jan discovered that Tony's literary tastes and hers were remarkably similar. She liked history, and so did he, judging from the excellent titles dealing with every phase of world events from the Romans through the Vietnam conflict. She loved geography, and Tony's library housed books about every corner of the earth.

It filled her with a precious sense of security to curl up in the largest of the leather chairs, which she fancied was Tony's favorite, and turn the pages of books she knew he had held before her. Whenever she came upon marked passages or marginal notes in Tony's strong, bold script, she read them greedily, thrilled at the insights they gave her into his private thoughts.

One evening, curled up in the middle of the room in "Tony's chair" reading a history of the counts of Borromeo, Jan drifted off to sleep, and soon she was involved in a frustrating dream in which she searched endlessly for Tony through the dark and intricate passages of an ancient castle.

Time and again she caught sight of him . . . called out . . . ran toward him . . . Each time his arms opened for her, and though she rushed toward him eagerly, he always vanished again before she could reach him. Finally, awaking with a start half an hour later, she tried in vain to shake off the queasy, alarmed feeling that slid over her like a cold hand. *A remnant of the dream,* she tried to reassure herself, and then with a terrifying prickle up her spine she realized her uneasiness sprang from the fact that she was no longer alone.

The book tumbled out of her lap. She froze. Then with a tremulous half whisper she reached out through the circle of light illuminating the room only a foot or two beyond her chair. "Who's there?"

A soft chuckle answered and then a low-timbred voice. "Who were you expecting?"

Weak with relief, Jan recognized the voice as Tony's, and as he stepped into the lamplight, she could barely stifle the glad cry that crowded her throat. How golden he looked! How virile and appealing . . .

A sardonic smile passed over his lips. "This must be fascinating," he said, stooping to retrieve the book. "I'd begun to believe you were in a coma."

He held a drink in his hand, she saw, and it was plain from the intimate way he was staring at her that he had been watching her for longer than she cared to imagine.

With a dry mouth, she said, "When did you arrive?"

"Long enough ago to tire of waiting for you to wake up," he answered. He came around the table and took a seat beside her.

"Ah—the Isola Bella," he said, flipping through the pages she had fallen asleep over. "The island home of the Borromeos." He set his drink aside and fixed his gaze upon her. "Were your dreams as enchanted as it?"

Remembering the tortuous nightmare from which she had just awakened, she answered weakly, "Hardly."

His gaze moved over her, touching her as if his eyes were the strong, slender fingers that rested on the chair's arm. "This is how you spend your evenings?" he murmured. "Reading?"

Breathless, Jan nodded. She could hardly believe he was here. He was so near she had only to put out her hand to meet his flesh. An animal warmth seemed to radiate from him, and his arms, muscled and bare below the short sleeves of his thin silk shirt, gleamed sensuously in the lamplight. Dizzy with love for him, she heard herself say faintly, "You've been away for a very long time."

A swift change came over his face. His gaze darkened, and she heard the quickening of his breath. "I needed time to think."

About what? A piercing pain stabbed through her. *Her work? Had he come here to dismiss her?*

Then his voice sounded again, this time as measured and quiet as the ticking of the clock. "You see," he said, "I've fallen in love with you, Jan."

Her breathing stopped. *In love with her.* She could only stare.

"Is that such a terrible thing?" he said lightly in response to her look of shock. But his jawline hardened, and through her dazed bewilderment Jan saw the lean lines of his body tense.

She found her voice. "What? What did you say?"

"I said I love you."

Incredible. Unbelievable. She spoke out sharply. "I won't play games with you!"

"I haven't asked you to."

"Then what do you want?"

"I want you to love me, too," he answered without hesitation. "And I'm convinced that you do."

This was another trick. A cruel, heartless trick to make a fool of her again. Jan sprang up from her chair, but Tony rose more swiftly and gathered her to him with his powerful arms. His lips came close to hers. "Say something."

"What do you expect me to say?" She gasped. "Think of how we parted!"

"I've thought of nothing else for weeks. You looked so tired, so ill."

"No!" The cry broke from her throat. "I mean on the mountain! The things you said to me—"

She felt his body harden against her. "Sit down. I see we have to talk."

"What will we say?" Her eyes flashed angrily. "Will you remind me again of how willing I was? That's what you're hoping will happen now, isn't it? You're hoping that if you tell me you love me I won't be able to resist you, that I'll offer myself to you again."

His gaze seared her like a branding iron. "I would welcome making love to you," he muttered hoarsely. "God knows I've wanted to long enough. But I want you to want it, too." His eyes took on a bright, ironic glitter. "I want you to know exactly where you stand."

"I know that now!" she came back hotly, cut to the quick by his sarcasm. "You think you bought and paid for me when you transferred my clothing bills to the silk firm."

A muscle rippled in his jaw. "A small thing. And I had two reasons for doing it. For one, you had no money; and for another, it was the simpler way of handling the matter since you are unfamiliar with the monetary exchange. I did not"—he eyed her stonily—"buy and pay for you."

Her voice rose. "You lured me up to those mountains to make a fool of me."

"Maybe I did." His unwavering gaze held her. "I'm not sure what my motives were then. I do know," he added no less sternly, "that I resented being backed into a corner—particularly when I wasn't ready for you."

A vivid flush stained her cheeks. "You're saying *I* tried to seduce *you?*"

"I am saying"—he tightened his embrace—"that we were two people responding naturally to the tumult of our emotions. What I wasn't ready for was to admit that you'd become so important to me that the idea of a cheap affair with you was repugnant."

Jan's lips flew apart. "You could never have had one—no matter *what* you wanted!"

"I am aware of that." He brought her roughly to him. "I understand quite clearly now why you behaved as you did—and I understand why I acted as I did, too. So we need waste no more time in quarreling and recriminations. There's no ground now on which we can't agree."

Jan stared up at him incredulously. "Do you

actually think you can smooth away all the pain you've caused me with a few easy sentences?"

His blue eyes glittered. "I've caused you pain? Then you do love me."

"You hurt my pride! That has nothing to do with love!"

"Doesn't it?" Suddenly he swung her up into his arms. "I'm never going to let you go, Jan," he said thickly. "You belong to me."

"Maria belongs to you!"

"I am not in love with Maria."

"You're going to marry her!"

"I intended to, yes." Sensing that, despite Jan's anger, she would listen to him now, he let her body slide slowly down his thighs until her feet touched the floor. Aroused by the contact so long denied, a fire leaped simultaneously between them and for a moment they stood locked together in a smoldering haze of desire.

Jan turned aside first. "Finish with this," she said as soon as she could control her voice. "It's late. I'm tired."

"I'm tired, too," he said firmly, placing his hands on her shoulders and turning her toward him again. "I'm tired of pretending . . . tired of longing for you and never having you . . . tired of searching for happiness where it doesn't exist. I've had the devil's own time coming to terms with my love for you, my darling." He stared straight into her eyes. "We're such an unlikely pair. How did we ever fall in love?"

Jan's throat tightened. She knew exactly how she had fallen in love with him. Though she had known him for only a brief time, he was flesh of her flesh, blood of her blood. He was made for her, and she could claim him now—if only she dared trust him.

"What about Maria?"

"Maria and I are perfectly suited to each other," he said calmly. "Same background, same friends, same past experiences."

Jan's heart lurched. The same *physical* experiences! *They are lovers,* she thought hotly, *and yet he is offering himself to me!*

"Maria is poised, elegant, sophisticated," he went on unrelentingly. "Visibly, she would seem an asset to any man."

Jan broke in harshly. "What kind of speech is this? You claim to be in love with one woman and in the same breath you're praising another!"

"Let me finish. None of those things that I formerly found attractive in Maria and that I thought essential to my happiness seem important now."

Jan scoffed. "You expect me to believe that?"

"Why shouldn't you?"

"You arrogant male!" Jan's voice broke. "Your word is law, you think. You've *said* it—therefore it is!" Angry tears rolled down her cheeks. "Ever since the day I stepped off the plane with you you've criticized me—my hair, my enthusiasms, the books I read—"

He gazed at her. "Don't forget your aunt."

Another flood of tears spilled over her lashes. "Oh—if you knew how much I hate you . . . !"

In one swift motion he swept her into his arms, pressing her wet face to his chest and whispering thickly, "My poor, beautiful, foolish baby. When will you ever learn to value yourself? The world *is* your oyster, my darling. You have everything—you *are* everything I could ever desire. You haven't the least idea how wonderful you are. Today in the silk houses of Como, of Paris, of Milan, your name is on every lip—and look at you." He kissed the tears from her cheeks. "Desolate because you envy Maria, who hasn't a grain of talent or originality in the whole of her."

Jan wrenched herself from his arms. "I do not envy Maria! I wouldn't be like Maria Bertani for all the Antonio Torellis in Italy!"

Tony's laughter rang clear. "There's only one, my love." He brought her to him again in a fierce hug. "And there's only one of you, and you belong to me. Promise me you'll never change a hair on your head."

A dam of self-restraint broke inside Jan. "You don't love me!" she wailed.

He chuckled softly in her ear. "You'll never convince yourself of that, my darling. You love me too deeply, you want me too badly." He felt her stiffen, and he tightened his embrace. "You can't hide it, Jan—and there's no need for you to try. Can't you see that I love you in exactly the same way? Open your heart to me, Jan. Listen there to what I'm saying." He bent and kissed her salty lips. "I want you to marry me."

"*Marry* you—" The room seemed to suddenly upend itself. "You want to marry me?"

"Of course, you adorable goose. What do you think I've been saying?"

Every inch of her body trembled. "Wild, crazy, wonderful things," she whispered in a dazed voice.

157

"But you must take them back, Tony. You must take them back now before I begin to believe them. You can't want to marry me. I really am prim, prissy Miss Martin." She gulped back her tears. "I'm all those things that irritate you so."

He kissed her again, tenderly. "You are all those things that have become so dear to me," he murmured against her hair. "What a complicated little thing you are. I wonder how many lifetimes will be required for me to plumb those secret, fiery, passionate yearnings you've taken such care to bury within you."

She was dreaming.

But no—the breath hot against her cheek was Tony's breath, the arms that held her, Tony's arms. He was alive and real, and he loved her! "Are you sure, Tony?"

"Judge for yourself," he said thickly and found her mouth with his. Leaning into the taut hardness of his body, she heard her own heartbeat in tune with his, and doubt—of no more substance than a morning mist—lifted and dissolved in the heat of Tony's lips moving on hers.

Chapter Fourteen

Tony took Jan to Isola Bella.

It was to have been a honeymoon trip that he planned after he left her the night he discovered her asleep with the romantic history of the counts of Borromeo in her lap, but Jan said no to that, reluctantly but firmly.

"I love you—yes! With all my heart. And of *course* I want to marry you, but not yet, Tony," she told him a few days later. "We are seeing each other in a new way now. I'm not used to it. I'm not sure you are, either." Her eyes clouded. "Give us time, Tony. Give *yourself* time to be absolutely sure."

"I've been absolutely sure for days," he answered her hoarsely. "I don't want to wait."

But in the end he had allowed her to have her way and summoned the Mignellis—Roberto and Angela—to meet them at Isola Bella for a week and act as chaperones until they went from there to Como where Jan's designs would be shown for the first time to an international gathering of buyers.

"Everything will be as proper as if Aunt Elizabeth herself had arranged it," Tony grumbled when the Mignellis had agreed to join them at Isola Bella.

Jan laughed at his chagrin. "I'm glad we're doing things in a way she would approve of. Aunt Elizabeth was very stiff and conventional, but she was a lady, and I'd like to think that I'm one, too."

"Of course you are," said Tony, but he growled the words into the hollow of her throat as if he were about to eat her. "As ladylike a wanton as ever breathed a lustful breath."

"Tony!" She knew he was teasing, but she was still sensitive about the remarks he had made to her on the mountain and very much aware of how easily her passions were aroused when he held her in his arms. It was this as much as anything that had warned her to delay their marriage.

Tony was a vibrant, hot-blooded man, and obviously, beneath her generally subdued exterior, she herself was an erotic, passionate woman. They needed a cooling-off period, she felt, a time in which to be certain that there was more to the attraction that had drawn them together than mere physical desire.

"And another thing," she told him one morning beside the pool. "According to what you've told me, suddenly I am a great success. My work when it's shown in Como will create a sensation in the silk world. I need time to get used to that, too."

When Tony had told her as he held her in his arms the night he proposed that her name was on the lips of every silk merchant in the fashion capitals of Europe, she had been too enthralled with his declaration of love to absorb anything else that he was saying. But later, alone in her bed and wide awake with the excitement the evening had brought, the full impact of his words had hit her with the shock of a brick falling on her head.

All her worries about her designs being failures had been for nothing! All her worries about Tony had been for nothing, too.

This sudden outpouring of blessings descending upon her without warning left her for days in a mild state of shock. Each time she looked up and saw Tony at her side, each time she touched his hand or turned on her finger the emerald set in a circlet of diamonds that he had given her the morning after his proposal, she had to begin all over again reassuring herself that what had happened was real.

The ring was not an engagement ring, Tony told her firmly when he produced it from the villa safe as magically as everything else had occurred since his return. The engagement ring he would choose later for her alone. The emerald, he said, was a betrothal gift, an heirloom that the eldest Torelli male had traditionally presented to his bride-to-be since 1647.

To Jan it was far more than just a gift, albeit a very special one. The ring seemed to tell her more clearly even than Tony's words that he had definitely made up his mind that he loved her and wanted to spend the rest of his life with her. It proved that he ranked her with the women who had brought honor and beauty to his family for generations, and she was overcome by the wonder of that. For a few minutes after he had slipped it on her finger, Jan hovered on the verge of giving in to his wish that they be married at once.

But then her better judgment had reasserted itself, and together they had altered Tony's "honeymoon" plans to include the Mignellis and turned the trip into a romantic interlude prefacing their marriage.

Isola Bella, rising from Lake Maggiore, captured Jan's imagination as nothing else she had seen in Italy, an effect that, she admitted, might be due partly to the fairytale turn her own life had taken. Any place where Tony was would be a magic spot, but still Isola Bella fit so perfectly into the fantasy world in which she was suddenly living that it seemed to have been designed especially for her rather than for Count Carlo Borromeo's fair Isabella.

Beginning with Carlo, the island—once a barren rock—had been transformed, and after several centuries of Borromeo influence it had become an island of mystical enchantment covered with exotic gardens in which grew plants and flowers from all over the world. The soil in which they thrived had been transported bit by bit from the mainland in accordance with Carlo's vision of turning the island into a green, growing replica of a ship. The terraced gardens he designed to resemble the prow and the superstructure of the vessel as well as to screen with their greenery the enormous palace which he put into construction in the midst of them.

"Carlo died before the palace was finished," Tony told Jan the evening they approached it through a milky mist.

Jan was already aware of that. It was Carlo's endeavors about which she had been reading when she fell asleep in Tony's library, but she was wise enough now to keep silent and to listen contentedly as Tony described in his own way the lavish palace completed by Carlo's son.

During the week that followed, she and Tony and the quiet, unassuming Mignellis lived in opulent splendor. Though most visitors to the island were allowed only glimpses of the elaborately decorated rooms of the palace, a long-standing acquaintance-ship between the Torellis and the Borromeo heirs afforded Tony the privilege of lodging there whenever he chose and with whomever he liked as his guests.

Through the midday hours, while the island was packed with tourists, the four of them retreated to the suite provided them in the upper reaches of the palace. They played card games together and chatted, and of course they dined together, but the Mignellis were considerate and discreet chaperones and left Tony and Jan ample time alone to explore the depths of their newly discovered love—and to unwind as well the twists and turns of their earlier relationship.

"You were such a prig, I thought," Tony scolded frankly. But his strong fingers stroked with gentle tenderness the nape of Jan's neck as he spoke, and the movement softened his words.

"I despised your arrogance," Jan retorted heatedly, and then they both collapsed in laughter.

"You were too quick to take offense," Tony criticized.

"Because you were so offensive!" Jan taunted. But the old irritations only seemed to draw them closer now.

In the early morning hours before the tourists arrived, they wandered hand in hand through the miles of dewy gardens, breathing the exotic fragrances of the flowers and marveling at the fascinating designs and lavish collections of trees and plants spread out over ten terraces. One Jan particularly loved contained a pool of giant water lilies standing several feet tall and spreading their foot-wide pink blossoms over the still, green water like fluted umbrellas.

In the evenings, when the hordes of awed visitors had departed again, she and Tony—and sometimes the Mignellis, too—made their own private tours of the castle's high-ceilinged rooms, admiring the paintings and statuary and—where Tony and Jan were concerned, at least—admiring each other.

Only one small cloud marred the otherwise perfect sky that looked down on Jan's enchanted world: Tony said nothing of Maria.

At first she had been pleased by that. Then it occurred to her that there was a kind of unnaturalness in the way Tony skirted every topic that might include the woman he had once thought to marry, and she grew uneasy. When she lay between the linen sheets in her elegant bedroom on the opposite side of the suite from Tony's, her imagination often produced Maria's shrewlike countenance.

Where was she? Jan hoped with all her heart that Tony had told Maria that he planned to marry Jan, and most nights lying in the darkness she persuaded herself that that was so. That was why Tony had nothing to say about Maria, she reasoned. Their parting had been unpleasant, and he wished to forget about it. Generally she could fall asleep then, but the next night Maria's face would loom once more and she would have it to do all over again.

On the last day of their stay on Isola Bella, Tony rose before dawn and went down into the gardens. When Jan awoke, he was standing by her bed with a breakfast tray, and on it lay a nosegay of cinnamon-scented dianthus and dewy pink rosebuds.

"Today we leave for Como," he announced.

His voice was crisp, but behind his heavy-lidded eyes Jan could see desire leap like a flame, and self-consciously she slid the sheet up over her thinly covered breasts.

He set the tray on the table and knelt beside her. "Jan," he said thickly. "Roberto and Angela are down in the gardens—"

Jan ran her tongue across her lips. "No, Tony— please. Everything has been so lovely. Let's not spoil it now with recklessness—"

"Not spoil it—seal it," he said urgently. He took her face between his hands and touched her lips with his. "I want you, Jan—I need you."

Desire, matching his, flared up within her. "Oh, Tony—"

"Make room for me, Jan—in your heart, in your bed—"

He lay down beside her, sliding his arm beneath her shoulders, lifting her to his chest with a barely stifled moan. They kissed. Jan felt the fire of his ardor inflaming her, felt her mouth go slack with passion, her breathing deepen— But a stifled cry broke from her. "Tony, I'm frightened—"

He drew back, startled.

"It frightens me that we need each other so." The words spilled from her. "Is this all we have? Is this raking need the substance of our love? When it's satisfied, will there be nothing left?"

With a burst of husky laughter he crushed her to him, covering her face again with his kisses— covering her throat, her breasts. "Oh, my lovely, foolish darling, this is only the beginning."

"Then let's wait, Tony!" She pushed her palms against his chest and separated herself from him. "I love you so much. With every fiber of my being I love you. I want perfection when we come together. I want ours to be a joining of heart and mind and soul as well as of our bodies. Can't it be that, Tony? Can't it?"

He looked at her for an instant. Then he rose and went to the window. Finally he turned back to her, and relief sharper than the pain that cut at her throat from her stilled breath washed over her. He was smiling. He came toward her.

"Yes, Miss Martin," he taunted softly, but there was laughter in his eyes. "Whatever you want is what you shall have."

Jan came up on her knees in the bed and flung her arms about his waist. "Oh—I love you!"

"Then have a little care," he warned with good-natured gruffness. "My intentions are good but they're thin as paper." At the door he turned back to look at her. "You're beautiful. Did I tell you that?"

There were stars in her eyes. "No."

He made a move toward her. "Beautiful . . . desirable—and devilishly inviting in that damned transparent nightgown!"

"Tony!" She yanked the sheet up to her neck, but he came no closer and, laughing, said over his shoulder, "Get dressed. The launch is leaving at eleven."

Chapter Fifteen

Jan wore her madras suit into Como and a pair of white stilt heels that Tony had surprised her with from Jean LeCou's the day they left for Isola Bella.

She had forgotten that Como was such a bustling city. Or perhaps, she reflected, as she and Tony were being driven toward the silk firm, it was the contrast of the hum and hurry of the traffic to Isola Bella's isolated tranquility that she was noticing.

Glancing across at Tony, absorbed now in papers from his briefcase, she felt contentment spread through her like fine wine. Everything in her life was perfect. Tony loved her. She would soon be his wife. And her design work had come into fruition as well.

According to Tony, the response to her first set of designs was unprecedented. More buyers had accepted invitations to the Torelli Silks showing than ever before in the company's history. When she walked into the showroom today, Tony had warned her, she must be prepared to step into the spotlight.

It was odd, she thought, that only a few weeks ago she would have been terrified at such a prospect, but now, with Tony at her side and secure in his love, she felt there was nothing she could not handle. The power of love! How had she survived without it?

Her musings came to an abrupt end as the Rolls pulled up in front of Torelli Silks and the chauffeur sprang out to assist them from the car.

Tucking his papers inside his case, Tony smiled at Jan and gave her hand a squeeze. "Ready?"

"Ready—and eager," she said with a smile of her own.

"Ah, that's my girl," he told her proudly. But when he had helped her out, he hesitated on the curb. "There's one thing, Jan—"

Her heart stopped. "What is it? What's wrong?"

"It's about Maria."

Maria. Jan swallowed. "Will she be here?"

"I'm sure so, and I want to tell her the first moment I can what our plans are."

In the days they had spent at Isola Bella, Jan had almost convinced herself that Tony had privately contacted Maria and that she was out of their lives forever. Now she saw what a naïve idea that had been. Of course Maria had to be faced by both of them—and the sooner the better. Jan lifted her chin. "I'm glad she'll be here. When will you speak to her?"

"Before the bidding starts, I hope."

"How will she react, do you suppose?"

Tony set his jaw and moved with Jan toward the

brass door of the silk house. "I think she'll be furious. Or else she will refuse to believe me. Maria's quite good at hiding from herself the things she doesn't choose to face. It may take her a while to accept what has happened, and she may get nasty in the meantime . . ." He forced an assured smile and slipped his arm around Jan's waist. "But don't spoil your day worrying about it. I want you to enjoy yourself. You'll have many successes grander than this one, my darling, but none will ever be quite as sweet as the first. Nothing must be allowed to mar it."

Tony was right on all counts. Jan was swept into the spotlight at once. It was a splendid, unbelievable afternoon—and Maria was definitely nasty.

Jan knew that Tony had spoken to Maria as soon as she saw her elegantly dressed rival seated rigidly in front of the fashion ramp as the crowd was gathering in preparation for a final courtesy showing of designs from rival houses—a kind of preview for the next commercial showing in West Berlin.

When Maria saw Jan looking at her, she sent a venomous stare across the space that divided them. Jan reacted as if a snake had slithered up her backbone, but in spite of her revulsion her heart twisted in pity for the haughty, elegant beauty who looked so unhappy. Jan knew the pain unrequited love could bring, and even though Maria had used her badly in the past, she felt a surge of sympathy for her.

But Jan quickly forgot Maria when Tony slipped into the chair beside her just as the lights were coming down for the start of the show. "You can relax now," he murmured, taking her hand. "All the bids are in. The day was ours."

"You're pleased?"

"Pleased!" He chuckled softly. "You innocent—you've turned the earth upside down with your clever fingers. Don't you know that? We've sold enough silk today to wrap the world six times. When this is over, Miss Jan Martin, you and I are going to celebrate."

"What about Maria?" she whispered.

"She took the news far better than I expected." Jan saw his eyes linger for a moment on Maria's haughty profile. "I'm surprised, though, that she's still around. Normally I would have imagined she'd go off somewhere to sulk."

Jan's gaze followed his, but this time she found Maria's grim demeanor more frightening than piti-ful. There was something in the proud set of her shoulders that set Jan's heart thumping—as if Maria were a cat crouched before a baited trap.

She shivered, and Tony turned to her with imme-diate concern. "Chilly? I can have the air condition-ing cut back—"

"No, no—I'm fine." But even after the lights were lowered, and the first model had stepped upon the ramp in a shimmering dazzle of diaphanous silk, Jan's uneasiness persisted.

The showing of Tony's competitors' silks went on for a long while, and gradually Jan relaxed. Her creative imagination was stimulated by the work of her competitors, and in time she found her fingers

171

itching to get hold of a sketching pencil.

It was true, she realized with a sense of humble wonder, that in that endless night when she had worked to exhaustion to produce the dozen new designs for Tony to bring to Como she had been blessed with a special breakthrough in her talent. The designs that were being paraded before her now were outstanding, but her own, which had been grabbed up so eagerly by the buyers, were sparked with a special little flair, a twist of creative genius she could claim no credit for because it had been wrung from her unwittingly. But once the breakthrough had occurred, her work had been forever changed. The flair was intrinsic to it.

In her fury with Maria that day by the pool at the Villa Torelli, she had vowed to use as her logo the mouse from Kansas. But now, she saw with satisfaction, no logo was needed. The buyers who this morning had seen the results of those agonizing hours of work would recognize her mark instinctively wherever her future designs were shown. In the darkness of the showroom, she experienced a profound sense of gratitude that so precious a gift was hers. Automatically her fingers went to the armoire key dangling from its chain at her throat, and she thought with additional thanksgiving of how fortunate she was that the accident of losing the portfolio had prevented her from giving Tony work that she now recognized as less than her best.

Bemused, she let her attention drift. Then all at once she felt Tony stiffen at her side. Her glance flew to his face and she saw a look of angry astonishment blazing in his eyes.

Following their glare, her own eyes leaped to the last model who had appeared on the ramp, a statuesque blonde who wore, for the West German firm she represented, a loosely flowing caftan done in subtle tones of gold, green, and purple on a white background. But what caught Jan's eye and held it in paralyzed astonishment was the design.

It was a graceful intertwining of grape leaves, wheat, and violets.

Drawing a sharp breath, she turned to Tony. "That's mine!" she whispered incredulously.

He met her gaze with blue eyes turned to steel. "Of course it is," he snapped. "Do you think I'm blind?"

"But how—?" Jan's attention jumped again to the stage. But just then there was a burst of applause. The lights came up. The show was over.

"Tony—" She turned to him and met his ice-blue glare.

"You sold me out," he said through tight lips.

"No, Tony! I'm as shocked as you!"

"You brazen tramp," he said thickly. "In my own showroom—" White with fury, he wheeled about and made his way rapidly through the crowd. Jan started after him, but a cold hand gripping her elbow stopped her. Turning, she saw Maria's tawny eyes burning across at her with vengeful delight.

"That last little outfit was a fitting end to your day of triumph, wasn't it?" she said.

"You stole that sketch!" Jan hissed.

"Of course I did." Maria smiled. "But who will ever believe that?"

"Tony will!"

173

"Don't be absurd. I saw how he looked at you. He'll never believe anything you say again."

"He won't listen to you! He loves me. We're going to be married."

"You *were* to be married. I doubt very much that will happen now."

Jan's voice struck out at her. "What are you trying to do? Ruin your own company?"

"You don't give a fig about the company," answered Maria sharply.

"Neither do you, obviously. But Tony does. If you cared anything at all for him, you could never have betrayed him."

Maria's limpid eyes narrowed to slits. "My feelings for Tony are no concern of yours. He belonged to me before you came, and he'll be mine again when you're gone."

Jan's voice rose as the crowd flowed away from them. "But why are you doing this? Why do you want to humiliate him?"

Maria's expression hardened. "Everything is so simple to you, isn't it? Black-and-white loyalties. Right and wrong. Why you haven't bored Tony to insanity I'll never know." In a cloud of expensive perfume she swept past Jan. "Go back to Kansas, little girl. This is our world—Tony's and mine. You don't belong here."

Watching her go, Jan stifled a cry. *You're wrong! I do belong here! I belong with Tony.*

In a few minutes, however, when Jan was finally able to thread her way through the mob jamming the corridors and enter Tony's office, she realized with stunned despair as soon as she saw his face that Maria was right. She was not a part of Tony's world, and he no longer wanted her in it.

His gaze, lighting on her as she passed through the doorway, was stony and uncompromising. "Say what you have to say," he commanded, "and then get out."

Jan stared at him. "You've already made up your mind, haven't you?"

"The design you filched and sold to West Germany made it up for me," he said curtly. Then, with deliberate rudeness, he swiveled around in his chair and faced the window that looked out over the Piazza Cavour.

"You've invited me to speak," Jan said through a tight throat. "May I at least have your attention?"

"You have it."

"Then look at me!"

Angrily he whirled about. "To be quite honest, the sight of you sickens me."

The impact of his words all but flattened her, but with a desperate will she held on to her poise. "I can understand why you would feel that way if you believe I have dealt behind your back."

"You surely won't deny that was your design the model was wearing."

"Certainly not. I've already acknowledged that it was. Besides that, you saw it yourself the first day you examined my work." *The day you kissed me for the first time,* her heart cried out, but she went on firmly. "It was one of the sketches I prepared for you to take to Como."

"It was not," he denied flatly.

"It was not one I *gave* you—and for a very good reason," she went on patiently, though her blood was racing. "When the time came to make up the portfolio, that sketch and more than a dozen others were missing from my studio."

Tony's lip curled. "Oh, I see. They were stolen, of course."

"Yes." She paused. "By Maria."

"Maria!" The color drained from his face. "You have cheapened yourself enough already. Must you discredit Maria, too?"

"She admitted it, Tony!"

His purple-blue eyes turned stormy. "You can't have a hope I would ever believe such a ridiculous lie—and coming from one so prim and proper, too," he taunted viciously. "What would dear Aunt Elizabeth say?"

Suddenly Jan was furious. "What matters is what *I* say, what *I* think! You have held me in your arms. You have kissed me and told me that you love me. You've asked me to marry you and given me this—" She pulled the emerald ring from her finger and sent it spinning across the polished surface of the desk. "*Those* were lies, Signor Torelli!"

White-faced, Tony picked up the ring and thrust it into a drawer. "Maria warned me about you from the first. I saw bumbling naïveté. She saw malice."

"Certainly she should know how to recognize it!"

Tony glared. "Naturally I am dismissing you. The money owed you for the designs that were sold today will be placed in escrow in a Milan bank until such time as it can be safely determined that they, too, have not been pirated to other markets."

"That can be determined right now!" said Jan, shaking with rage. "I have neither sold nor given any of my work to anyone but you. You have tricked me and insulted me, but I will not allow you to cheat me in the bargain! You will pay me what you owe me now, or I will go to the police."

Her threat surprised Tony, and he smiled in spite of his anger. "It might be worth allowing that, just to watch what would happen." Then his amusement vanished abruptly, and he leaned across the desk with a penetrating look that shot straight through her. "I will give you half of what I owe you now for the name of your accomplice."

Jan's jaw dropped. "My *accomplice!*"

"Give me the name of whoever is siphoning off the top work from my firm, and you can walk out of here and be in Paris by six o'clock this evening with money in your pockets."

"Why, you blind, arrogant—*executive!* I gave you that name—free!"

"Maria?" His look was contemptuous. "You're blaming Maria because when you made up your mind to marry the Torelli fortune, you found Maria in the way."

Tears of anger and humiliation sprang up in Jan's eyes. "You can believe that if you want. But you'll soon discover that Maria didn't steal my sketches simply to make me look bad in your eyes. I'm sure that until today it never occurred to her that I was serious competition for your attentions."

For the first time a flicker of doubt appeared in Tony's eyes, but he allowed it to remain for only a moment. "Maria has always been jealous of you."

"Only as much as she would be of any woman you so much as spoke to. I'm leaving, but that won't stop her from her maniacal pilfering. When you finally wake up enough to realize the truth of what's happening, I hope you remember that you were warned."

Tony's jaw hardened. "Your plane ticket will be waiting for you in Milan. The Rolls is ready now to take you there. Whatever you left at the villa will be forwarded to you in Paris."

"That's fine with me!" said Jan with flashing eyes. "But there's one more detail." Catching hold of the armoire key dangling from her neck, she gave it a jerk and snapped the narrow silver chain. "Here!" She flung it across the desk. "I thought I had locked up my treasures, but they are trash because of Maria. Nevertheless, they belong to you—and you're welcome to them. They'll be of no commercial use, but perhaps you can frame one or two"— her voice broke—"just as a reminder that even the great Black Prince is not infallible!"

Chapter Sixteen

Jan had three hours to wait, she discovered when she reached the Milan airport, but she was so distraught by what had happened in Como that even the prospect of the lengthy delay made little impression upon her.

Numbly she sought out a seat in the crowded passenger lounge, and while her unfocused gaze moved over the travelers swarming around her, she relived every moment of the day that had begun so full of promise and ended so disastrously.

What if she had let Tony make love to her on Isola Bella? Would she be here now? What if she had married him when he had wanted? Would their love have been strong enough then, their ties so tightly binding that they could have weathered the traumas of this day?

Tony. It pained her even to think of his name. *And*

as for love— Tony had never loved her, or he would never have let her go, no matter how distraught he himself was. But for a brief moment her sympathies flew to him. The silk firm was so important to him—and he had trusted her. Then to be suddenly confronted with what appeared to be proof positive that she had betrayed him . . . That would be a crushing blow for any man—and for Tony, so self-assured, so accustomed to being in command, it must have seemed like the end of the world.

Then she remembered how unfair he had been. He had taken Maria's side at once, even though earlier he had warned Jan how unreasonable and nasty she could be. Tears blurred Jan's vision, and she turned her thoughts desperately to practical matters.

In her purse she had the sum of twelve dollars, and she had no place to stay in Paris. Stupidly, at the end of the first week at the villa she had terminated the lease on her flat. *But perhaps that was a good thing, after all,* she told herself wryly. *At least she had twelve dollars left from the refund!*

Probably she should have hauled Tony into court, just to watch him sputter! In time he would of course forward the money owed her. He was cruel and unforgiving, but at least he was honorable. In the meantime she could only hope that the stir her work had created in Como would enable her to find a job. Clothes she had plenty of. Wistfully she remembered the red organza and the crepe de chine dinner dress that she had worn only at Isola Bella. But at least, if worst came to worst, those were things of value she could sell.

Suddenly there was a quiet voice at her elbow. "Have you stopped speaking to me altogether?"

Startled, she whirled about. Tony stood beside her chair.

"I've spoken your name twice." His eyes rested darkly on her. "You seemed very far away."

Jan found her voice. "What are you doing here?"

He said solemnly, "Perhaps, like you, I am going to Paris."

She turned away. "Then you should be in the VIP lounge—not out here with the common folk."

A wry smile turned up his sensuous lips. "What an excellent idea." He caught hold of her arm. "Come along. We can talk there."

"I'm not going anywhere with you!"

"Oh, but you are." He took her wrist firmly, and when she started to protest, he said quietly, "Make a scene and we'll both be arrested."

"What do you *want?*"

Smoothly he moved her across the lobby. "For one thing, I've come to settle my debts; and for another, you have some explaining to do."

A harsh sound came out of her throat. "You missed your opportunity for that!"

Undeterred, he dragged her along the corridor until they came to a blue door marked PRIVATE.

The exquisitely decorated room he brought her into was empty, though a silver coffee service gleamed on a sideboard and a tray of pastries and fruit stood beside it.

"It's interesting," Tony said as he watched her reluctantly take a chair, "to observe how you've changed."

Jan only tightened her lips, and he went on in a pleasant tone. "Only a few weeks ago you were a trembling mass of nerves in this same airport, and now look at you." His tantalizing mouth curved slowly upward. "About to put on another of your famous pyrotechnic displays."

Jan jumped up. "If you've brought my money, give it to me! I'll miss my flight."

"Then miss it. You can take another."

"You inconsiderate tyrant!" she retorted bitterly. "You couldn't care less about anyone else's feelings, could you?"

"You are mistaken about that," he answered calmly and got to his feet. "Shall we have a cup of coffee together?" He moved toward the sideboard. "I'll even pour. That's considerate, isn't it?"

Seething, Jan sat down again. If she were meeting him for the first time, she thought, letting her gaze move with smoldering intensity over his supple form at the coffee bar, she would hate him for his arrogance. As it was, she only despised him for the way he had treated her—while every other unthinking part of her adored him!

Was she doomed to go through life melting inside each time she thought of his rugged brow or the curve of his mouth?

With trembling fingers she took the coffee cup he offered and set it down on a table beside her.

He passed her the food tray. "Something to eat?"

She shook her head, concentrating desperately on the jets rising effortlessly beyond the plate-glass window.

When Tony was seated again, he said in the same

casual tone as he had used to offer her the fruit, "You were correct. Maria is indeed the guilty party."

Jan's head swung around.

"Oh, I know," he said, smiling at her incredulous expression. "You told me that in Como."

"But you didn't choose to believe me!" she flung back acidly.

"I believe I would have—given a little more time. However, Roberto called immediately after you left."

Jan frowned. "Roberto Mignelli? What does he have to do with this?"

"There was something he wanted to tell me on Isola Bella, but he decided to check it out first." Tony set his coffee cup aside. "As you know, Roberto and Angela lead quite active business and social lives. They see everyone of importance who comes to Venice." He paused. "In the past few months they have seen Maria there eleven times."

Jan's heart began a slow pounding. "Perhaps she has a lover there," she said, amazed at her own spitefulness.

But Tony appeared unperturbed. "The Mignellis thought so, too—and that was why they hesitated to mention it to me on Isola Bella." His eyes moved over Jan. "You and I were so happy, and they were afraid the mention of Maria might cause friction."

When Jan was silent, he went on. "In Venice Roberto investigated. The man Maria was with"— he gazed directly at Jan—"was Helmut Dante, a

West German silk agent who Roberto has discovered has just been fired from the Dollary Company in Munich for illegally exchanging silk-screen rejects with a Taiwanese firm. Obviously he was Maria's partner in her little scheme."

Jan took a breath. "I see."

"But you aren't surprised."

"I'm surprised," she answered coldly, "that for Signor Mignelli two and two made four, but for you they only added up to three."

Tony laughed huskily, and a tremor of desire shook Jan. Quickly she averted her gaze. "It's also interesting," she said, "that you were willing to listen to him, but not to the woman you had asked to marry you."

For the first time since their quarrel had begun, Tony's assurance wavered, but he quickly recovered. "I have known Roberto and Angela for twenty-five years."

"And me for scarcely more than that many days," retorted Jan. She turned her gaze directly on him. "Since your faith relies on the passage of time rather than on what the heart dictates," she said cruelly, "what do you suppose went wrong in the case of Maria Bertani?"

An angry flush spread over Tony's face. "You would like an apology. Is that it?"

"Not at all. I can't rent an apartment with an apology or buy a loaf of bread or even a bus token." She got out of her chair. "I'd like my money, please, and then I'll say goodbye. This conversation, as far as I'm concerned, is over."

Abruptly Tony rose and, reaching inside his coat,

pulled out a thick white envelope which he passed across to Jan without a word.

She took it and, without inspecting its contents, thrust it into her purse. "When you see Maria," she said, turning toward the door, "give her my regards."

At once Tony's iron grip had hold of her arm and had swung her around. 'I've already seen Maria. She confessed to everything."

Jan was too surprised to speak.

"She was not interested, she informed me, in destroying the firm—and she was too selfish to see that was what was happening. All she cared about was turning the business into such an unrewarding, frustrating burden that I would soon reject it in favor of joining her on the social merry-go-round. In her eyes, the life of a playboy is the only suitable role for a man to play."

Jan stared at him. "She stole from you for such a ridiculous reason? I can't believe that!"

"No?" His dark brows arched. "Then perhaps you might find it less astonishing that I had difficulty believing *you!*"

Jan blushed. "Do you really mean to say that she went to such lengths merely to dampen your interest in the silk business?"

Tony gave a bitter laugh. "Dampen it? She intended to extinguish it. She was jealous." His hard gaze bored into her. "Have you ever been jealous, Miss Martin?"

Her color deepened. "You're hurting my arm."

He released his grip. "You're free to go now," he said bluntly, "but I would appreciate it if you would take a few more minutes to explain exactly how Maria gained access to your work."

Free to go. Jan's throat filled with a suppressed sob. She would never be that, but if she stayed one minute more she would make a worse fool of herself than she had already done in falling in love with him. "I have to go—my flight is leaving."

He jammed his hands into his pockets and stared across at her. "I will never prosecute Maria, but I feel I deserve the facts in the case."

"Let Maria tell you, then."

"She has." His voice grew husky. "But I would like to hear the truth from you."

Devil! thought Jan. In a minute she would be under his spell again. With one slow, sensual look and a catch in his voice he had aroused all the old passions. They were swarming about inside her like famished bees, and all she could think of was the harbor of his arms.

"If you miss your flight," she heard him say, "I'll fly you to Paris myself. Oh, yes," he said in response to her swift look. "I have a small jet. Two of them, in fact. And a castle on the Rhine." He took a step toward her. "Tomorrow I sign the final papers for an Alpine honeymoon cottage. All I need is you." His eyes glowed with a strange, tempting light she had never seen in them before. "Stay, Jan," he said thickly. "Not for ten minutes or ten years, but forever." His arms went around her waist. "Don't you know how much I love you?"

Her resistance crumbled. "Tell me, Tony," she whispered.

He pulled her roughly against him, his lips moving

in her hair, then down across her cheek until they found her mouth. They clung together, lifted by waves of longing that washed over them mercilessly.

"Wait!" Jan pulled away. Through the blood pounding at her temples Aunt Elizabeth's puritan logic had reasserted itself. "This is madness. Think, Tony, how you behaved toward me today. Think how *I* behaved. This isn't love."

"It *is,* my darling." He drew her to him again, the power of his arms pressing her breasts hard against his heart. "I can't live without you. I knew that two seconds after you left me."

"I wish I could believe that." She stared at him with shimmering eyes. "You want me because you know how much I want you, but I can't believe you love me."

His arms tightened. "Give me a chance to prove it."

She shook her head. "You're too volatile, too impetuous and vacillating." Her voice trembled. "And I'm too staid, too demanding. Maria told me I would bore you to insanity—I think she's right."

"You've already promised to marry me," he answered. Reaching into his pocket, he pulled out the emerald ring. "Here." He slid it on her finger and said hoarsely, "You're pledged to me."

"We broke that pledge, Tony—with our anger and our terrible accusations. Let me go."

"You can't leave," he said flatly, but he took his arms away. "You're under contract to Torelli Silks."

"So that's it! Business! That's all you care about."

"I care about your career, it's true. I care about the talent that can turn ordinary lines on paper into fluid images that no one can resist." He took her hands again. "But more than anything else I care about you, about the magic way you've brought together with your love all the separate parts of me," he went on. "I'm volatile, impetuous, vacillating." He pulled her to him. "But I can be tender, too." His lips moved on hers. "I have a great capacity for love," he said hoarsely, "but only you can unleash it. Stay, darling. Stay with me forever."

She felt the magnetism of his love drawing her to him. "Oh, Tony." Her arms went up around his neck. "I do love you. In spite of everything, I do—"

The room was quiet for a very long time. Finally Tony pulled away and, tracing her cheek with a gentle fingertip, he said in a teasing voice, "There's only one problem. We can't be married until September."

Jan drew back, wide-eyed, her face flushed with love for him. "Why not?"

"Because it's too late to be married in May."

Jan's laughter spilled over. "It's not too late for me. I'm not a shepherdess—and you're not a Premana ironmonger!"

"Don't you believe in tradition?" he said mockingly.

She nuzzled his neck with her lips. "Only when it suits me," she murmured. "And it definitely doesn't suit me to wait until fall to become your wife. Think of all the quarrels we might have."

"You'll be too busy working to quarrel," he chided. "When I called Allegra and told her to pack your things, she told me the studio was bare. Not a design in sight."

"They're all in the armoire," Jan said ruefully, withdrawing herself from his arms and settling in a red velvet chair. "And we can't use any of them because Maria has seen them all."

Tony sat down beside her and reached for her hand. "According to her, she took only a dozen to show to her merchant."

Jan nodded. "The ones in the portfolio that I had ready for you." She looked at Tony. "Maria's maid took them the day Maria had me drive her to the hairdresser."

Tony smiled. "The day you made your fabulous purchases at Jean LeCou's."

"When I got back to the tower Ann Janell was waiting outside with a huge shopping bag."

"Stuffed full of your work," said Tony.

"Yes. Actually, Allegra tried to tell me that Ann Janell had been up to my studio, but I misunderstood and thought she meant she'd only been to the tower to wait for me, and that wasn't news."

"Ann Janell took the sketches into Bellagio and gave them to Maria, I suppose," said Tony.

Jan laughed. "And ran out of gas on the way. I was to have filled up the car, but I was so bedazzled with my new dresses that I completely forgot."

Tony gave her a subdued look. "From Bellagio Maria went on to meet her buyer. She told me you almost ruined everything by taking so long to get home that day."

Jan blinked. "Maria told you all this?"

Tony smiled grimly. "She's quite proud of her expertise—particularly the skillful manner in which she returned your portfolio."

Jan bristled. "I suspected her that day, but I could find nothing missing after she left. What was really happening," she said ruefully, "was that while I was rounding up my designs from where she had scattered them all over the studio, she was down in my bedroom cramming the original portfolio behind the fire screen."

Tony's dark brows drew together. "You said all of the sketches are in the armoire. Even the ones Maria glimpsed briefly?"

Jan nodded.

"Then she can't have traded all of them off to the agent."

"Not unless she's more canny than I give her credit for. But even if the designs are safe, let's not use them." Jan got up and moved into Tony's lap. "Let's throw them away and start all over again with a brand-new slate."

"A brand-new sketchbook, my love," said Tony.

"And a brand-new life," answered Jan with shining eyes. They kissed. A departing jet roared overhead. When the room was still again, Tony said softly into her ear, "Let's go home, my darling."

ROMANCE THE WAY
IT USED TO BE...
AND COULD BE AGAIN

Contemporary romances for today's women.
Each month, six very special love stories will be yours
from SILHOUETTE.
Look for them wherever books are sold
or order now from the coupon below.

$1.50 each

Silhouette Romance